MW01103781

up,
down,
& sideways

by

Robert H. Patton

THE PERMANENT PRESS
SAG HARBOR, NY 11963

Copyright © 1997 by Robert H. Patton

Library of Congress Cataloging-in-Publication Data

Patton, Robert H.
   Up, down & sideways/by Robert Patton
     p.   cm.
   ISBN 1-877946-91-5
   I. Title.
  PS3566.A82612U6   1997
  813'.54 -- dc20   96-27409
                                       CIP

All rights reserved, including the right reproduce this book, or parts thereof, in any form, except for the inclusion of brief quotes in a review.

First edition, May 1997.

THE PERMANENT PRESS
Noyac Road
Sag Harbor, NY 11963

for Vicki, of course

and for B. V., with thanks

. . . to disintegrate on an instant in the explosion of mania
or lapse for ever into a classic fatigue.

W. H. Auden

When I was young my hobby was the weather. First thing each morning I would look to the sky for cloud types and to the lawn for frost or rain puddles. I checked the thermometer on my windowsill and the flying-horse weathervane atop the old carriage house, now a three-car garage, across the circular driveway. I recorded my findings in scholastic notebooks. The columns of data comprised a textbook I'd created, a manual not only of meteorology but of proper manual making. Even as an adolescent I presumed that my experience was instructive, a lesson others should heed.

Eventually I made my own weather predictions. In competing with TV professionals, I appreciated who were genuine aficionados and who were mannequins hired for their smiles and good hair. I rated them in my notebooks and occasionally sent fan letters, stamped and mailed by my father's secretary.

She must have said something, for my father began to criticize what he once had called sensible, evidently alarmed that I might actually become a weatherman. He set about altering the object of my fascination but not its habits, the research and analysis that were my main enjoyment. Soon he'd weaned me off weather and turned me on to the stock market. Rather than clouds, I would track the flow of money.

He bought me subscriptions to Value Line and several market newsletters. Annual reports appeared on my bedside table. In the evening we discussed stock picks. He favored blue chips. I liked new technologies with high P/E's, yet with huge potential to fly. I was sixteen then, in 1976. A conservative, I looked backward for direction. Today, almost twenty years later, I'm still a conservative, but with a twist: I know the past is what you make it.

Father opened an account for me at Tilton, Mayhew stockbrokers on Congress Street in Boston. Providing me ten thousand dollars to start investing with, he forbade me to buy on margin or to trade options short or long. My first three purchases were Wyant Computer, Digital Electronics, Merrill Lynch. I made a few hundred dollars but got bored with so little leeway to operate under Father's restrictions. I dumped my money into Shenandoah Oil at 26 and concentrated instead on losing my virginity, another tale of investment and yield whose payoff was a wash at best. A year later I persuaded my father to let me trade my account like a man.

I sold Shenandoah at 30, and with almost $20,000 in leveraged buying power was ready to start fresh. I'd noticed the emergence of drive-in/walk-up bank teller machines. Research turned up Diebold as a comer in the field. I got in under eight, and eventually owned 2,000 shares when the stock hit 87 in 1983. Damon was another success. My 2,200 shares rose from four bucks in 1980 to 38 in '83. Other winners were Drexler Technology, Minot Optics, U-Save Stores, cash-rich companies whose minimal debt made them strong in the face of high interest rates.

I scored with option calls on Bethlehem Steel during the worst of the Reagan recession. The steel industry was collapsing, but Bessie took steps, closing old factories, trimming the workforce, cutting away fat. The stock continued to tick down. Calls were trading at eighths. I bought more. The company announced a billion-dollar loss—the news I'd been waiting for, the bottom. When people started buying I tripled my money.

On the negative side, I had a stock go bankrupt in 1986, the year my father died. His doctor had fielded my questions about CAT scans with a tip on Alpha Partners, the patent holder on a portable breast scanner designed for home use and mobile clinics. Several hospital supply companies were looking to take the company over, he said. I bought in big. A good gambler pushes his luck when it's good, a bad gambler when it's bad. My luck had stunk for a while, yet when Alpha upticked a fraction I doubled my stake. The stock faltered. I averaged down, hoping for a home run. When the stock went belly-up, it left me worse than broke. Like market speculators who jumped out

Wall Street windows in 1929, I'd lost not what I had but what I didn't have. The money I'd sunk into Alpha was borrowed. I was glad my father wasn't there to see it.

He would have tried to help, admonished me with maddening rectitude before issuing a check. I'd endured his help the year before, when I'd been desperate for money and lawyers to bail me out of trouble. I'd suspected, during that low point in my life, that Father enjoyed my humiliation. I'd left the family under acrimonious circumstances several years earlier. My prosperity in exile had irritated him—just as, later, my personal and financial woes seemed to gratify him, to conveniently knot some last loose end in his life before he had to leave it.

My family is an old New England conglomerate, the getting of whose fortune we don't discuss. The family used to be better than it is today, by which I mean more industrious. The patriarchal name is Stalls. I'm a Halsey. On the Stalls family tree we Halseys are a twig and so must earn a living. The real money is nearer the tree trunk, doubled and redoubled through generations of prudent matrimony. Of my older relatives, some are working professionals, but most have yet to take a job. Instead they keep occupied. There are ladies busy in charity work, who garden, raise horses, ladies of a certain masculine handsomeness who consider dyed hair and painted fingernails the mark of idle minds. Their husbands often run whimsical businesses at serious deficits, millionaire owners of farm stands and marinas, art galleries and trout nurseries. Whittlers of duck decoys, breeders of foxhounds, they sell one or two a year and call it enterprise.

Inherited wealth has kept many Stalls men terminally young. Disguised as adults, they hold the attitudes of boys, childish or childlike depending on your politics. Browbeating a nephew, they display the brutality of the schoolyard. Over cocktails they may invoke some prep-school prejudice or a dusty theme like destiny or class to analyze what's wrong with

America. Then there are those Stallses whose total lack of professional accomplishment has opened their hearts to all the world's losers. Gentle and sad, they make no show of excellence. They sip twelve-year-old whiskey in ten-year-old tweeds and raise toasts to better men. "Finest kind!" they'll say when they hear of someone's triumph. "Keep it up!" You look for envy in their faces, a glimmer of loathing; it isn't there. Like happiness, success is something they can live without. They prefer the dream.

Any discussion of money bores them completely. They don't care where it comes from, they don't care where it goes. These are people who have never paid income tax. The family financial office does it for them, also pays their mortgages, their kids' tuitions, their servants' salaries. All their lives they have received quarterly income checks drawn from family cash funds. For years, my father, as head trustee at Stalls Associates, signed those checks. The office originally hired him as an accountant in 1952. At the time it was still managed by direct descendants of Samuel Stalls, the shipping magnate (and slave trader, if you must know). They'd refashioned Stalls Associates from an active business into a private investment firm, quietly tending the trust portfolios of Samuel's many beneficiaries.

As his example faded to myth, however, interest in finance waned within the family, prompting fears among the elder trustees that Stalls Associates might someday be Stalls in name only, its offices overrun with outsiders, its homey benevolence lost to the smiling contempt of MBA mercenaries for their overprivileged clients. Father's eventual appointment as head trustee put those fears to rest. He always had been popular with his employers. His status as a salaried tax mechanic evolved with each clambake and golf game into something approaching a partner. His marriage to my mother won him full acceptance. She was one-sixteenth Stalls. Their merger made him family.

He had no family of his own. To hear him talk you would have thought his life began in 1946, when he emigrated to the United States from Great Britain. His parents had been killed in the Blitz, he said, and he'd served in the British Army during World War II. His reticence about the past arose from belief that his foreign origins would keep him from the club, the Stalls fraternity; he even had recast his English accent into the regionless, formal intonations of a classical music deejay. Yet in later years he often purposely declared himself not a member of the Stalls family, not an equal, by letting slip suggestions of illegitimacy and childhood poverty. I wish I could say that he offered these hints to exalt his ascension from such difficult origins, or that his self-deprecation was a tactic to put others at ease. But in his office he received the heirs of Samuel Stalls with genuine deference, indeed with the breathless servility of a contented royal footman.

In private he allowed that some Stallses were less than perfect. They were spoiled, he said; clumsy with freedom. In the 1960s, when a number of my cousins became hippies and draft dodgers, he lamented what he called a failure of bloodlines (he was against the Vietnam War but in favor of sacrifice). When they returned in the 1970s, older and wiser and wondering about their inheritance, he embraced them as prodigal children. At Stalls family gatherings a favorite toast proclaims, "We're the best!" Father believed it. He believed it to his grave, which lies in ultimate assimilation in the Stalls family plot on Boston's North Shore, albeit in a corner.

I was born with two trust funds to my name, one technically termed a revocable trust, the other irrevocable, each worth about $100,000 in 1980 when I turned twenty. Dividends and interest on $200,000 are not enough to live on if you're thinking house and children and a comfy situation, plus any capital you spend cuts income even more. So in 1980 I went to my father requesting that the trusts be turned over to me, that I might manage them to suit my needs. I'd opened a new account with a discount brokerage and I wanted my money today. He was impassive. "Are you in trouble? Is it drugs?"

"I've read the terms of the trust. No explanation required."

"I'm asking as family, not your trustee."

"This is business," I said. "Family time was last month." While home on vacation last month, I'd announced to my parents that I was quitting college after the spring term of this, my sophomore year; my joke about us splitting the saved tuition hadn't amused them. "It's not drugs," I assured Father now. "Managing money is what I do best. To do it right, I need time and I need capital. This'll be my full-time job."

"Last month we agreed to a year off."

"To start."

Father, then sixty-one, was balding from the back of his head forward. He wore a square-cut suit and L. L. Bean walking shoes; the shoes identified him as a boss beyond dress codes. His office recently had been refurbished. Amid modular furniture and track lighting he seemed ensconced here through duty alone, a monk in a gallery of modern art. He said, "It's a pain moving these assets for so short a time. Why not trade through us?"

"I can do it cheaper through a discount house. And I want to keep my business private."

His eyebrows arched. "What sort of investments are you planning?"

"Market futures, options. Whatever it takes."

He considered. "No. I can't allow it."

I'd expected this; still it knocked me dizzy a moment. I pressed on, reciting the script I'd practiced. "You can't stop me. I'll sue for malfeasance."

"As your trustee I'm responsible for your financial welfare. If I believe you're jeopardizing that welfare, I must act against you." He paused. "I've seen it too often, Philip. Cousins who pissed their inheritance away on divorcees and religious gurus, on nutty save-the-world causes. Nat Stalls? When he was your age he gave half a million dollars to the American Civil Liberties Union. He sells cars now—a Stalls! His father has sat right where you're sitting and wept."

"Nat's a flake. I don't have a need to be poor."

"You want to be rich? You're rich already."

"Two hundred thou is nothing. It's a beginning."

"*One* hundred thou. The irrevocable's principle you can take only at my discretion."

"You'd withhold it?"

"I have to protect your issue."

"I don't have any issue!"

"Neither did your mother's father when he established the trust. Be glad he planned ahead."

"This is crap. I'll get a lawyer."

"My secretary can give you some names."

"I don't want one of your golf cronies. I want a sharp Jew who likes a fight."

He was silent a moment. "We won't fight. It's a business dispute between you and this office. The family needn't hear of it," he added, and my way to win was clear.

At a Stalls wedding reception soon thereafter, I cornered several cousins and informed them their wealth was disappearing. The stock market, I said, was in a long bear phase and everyone's worth was down. My cousins shrugged; their pockets were full enough. I quoted price declines, quoted the market doomsayers, columnists whose ill-invested readers crave company in hardship. I told them the wait-it-out policy of Stalls Associates was a sure slide to the poorhouse, still they were unmoved. What finally roused them was my naming of investment firms that did better, that through daring and diversification outperformed our family office. "No!" they exclaimed, for though they couldn't relate to dollars and cents, they could relate to competition, with its echo of the playing fields. I told them that's why I was leaving, pulling out my money—I cared about the score.

They confronted my father. From across the reception room I watched him in action. He touched their jacket sleeves as he spoke to them, calming their alarm. Over their shoulders his eyes met mine. My heartbeat felt like a fingertip jabbing under my breastbone, telling me to pay attention, be careful, beware. Then Father nodded tersely and turned his back to me.

I was scared of him, you see. I often wonder why. He wasn't coarse or domineering. He winced at violent confrontation. Yet his composure could seem clenched and barely contained, a willful put-on rather than his natural self. I wondered if his stern placidity was a self-administered antidote to some trauma in his youth—to his experiences in World War II, perhaps, and the memory of whatever bad things he'd seen or done. I understand some veterans compulsively display aggression in their postwar hobbies and demeanors. Not Father. His hands never closed to a fist. When angry, he'd flatten them in his lap or on the tabletop, like a cardsharp declaring his honesty.

Lofty in his professional status (Stalls Associates represented more than $500 million in assets), he was personally nondescript. Fiercely stubborn when he chose to be, he maintained a pose of passive awe before the Stalls escutcheon of old-world Anglican vanity. It was this contradiction that intimidated me, his manner of bland inscrutability that didn't square with the power he wielded. My pushy bravado in our recent exchanges was a kind of hysteria on my part, a petulant holding of breath until I turned blue. I was looking to get a reaction from him. He, as best I could tell from his non-reaction, was looking to see me smother myself.

At the wedding reception I imagined that his nod to me was a gesture of respectful surrender, for I'd taken our dispute where he wouldn't fight it, to the family. Within two months I'd wrested my inheritance from his control, and certainly his nod prefigured that concession. But penalties and fees he deducted beforehand bespoke the resentment he never showed. He was cool as a hangman. His nod merely meant goodbye.

My banishment from the family carried an outlaw glamor. It gave me identity and gave me a cause: I would succeed on my own, for spite. In dismantling my trusts, the office squeezed me for attorney's fees, a two-percent disbursement penalty, wiring costs, and broker commissions. The market was falling, so each day's delay, each day I couldn't sell, hurt. No family member had ever cut ties with Stalls Associates before. When word of my defection spread, my cousins were a little miffed, wishing me well while soothing Father with predictions of my failure. For twenty years he'd godparented their newborn and eulogized their dead, a sun and moon on their lives. They wanted no shadows, no change or disquiet. He was their invaluable servant, and a household collapses if the servants aren't happy. What guilt I felt about upsetting him was assuaged by his petty reprisals. As for my mother, though she was chagrined by the rift between her husband and only child, I confess I wasn't much moved. My years at boarding school and college had rendered her a bystander in my life. Our reunions always were a letdown to me, like seeing actors in the flesh.

Banishment implies a certain melodrama that was absent in my case. No curses or decrees came down, I just stopped going home. In subsequent years our continued proximity (I lived near my college in Providence, Rhode Island; Father was an hour's drive north, in Boston) emphasized the humdrum nature of our estrangement. The distance dividing us might as well have been an ocean, or the virtual moat a manicured lawn can be between two suburban homes. I spoke with Mother by phone and sometimes met her for lunch in Providence, when she rode the commuter train down. Attorneys handled my communications with Stalls Associates and the transfer of assets from its bank to mine. In time I received a wire of $185,000 and change. But my old account at Tilton, Mayhew remained a problem—established when I was sixteen, it was still in my father's name. I asked Mother for help in procuring the profits I'd earned the past four years. Certain our feud would end by Christmas, she rather playfully offered to petition Father on my behalf if she could tell him that I loved him. I told her it's a deal.

When spring classes ended, I rented a room above a pizza parlor just off campus. A note arrived on office stationery confirming an appointment with Mr. Halsey. I got my ear pierced the next day. I was nobody's kid anymore.

I dressed down for the meeting, baggy pants and two days' growth and naturally an earring. Outside Stalls Associates I bought flowers for my father's secretary. In six years with him, Doris Zuppa had contracted her employer's stately inscrutability: I judged her age around twenty-eight, her origins Italian or Spanish, her humor to be as prim as her dress. Her sexiness lay in its evident denial. In ambitious puberty I'd often fancied her having sex with me, and lately with my father. I was fitting him with flaws, some measly obsession to make him more lovable. The gentle patricide of deeming us equal was all that I was after, but still the cliché loomed: Some dads never die. "How charming," Doris said when I handed her the flowers.

Taking a chair in Father's office, I was confronted with my image. He'd recently redecorated. An oak-framed mirror hung on the wall behind his desk. When I gazed at him I saw his face—and my own, staring wide-eyed back at me from over his shoulder like a prankster in a group photograph. I looked like a rock star, moneyed and sloppy, also like a clown, the earring glinting in my lobe like a signal flash transmitting *idiot*, *idiot*, *idiot*. Father asked, "What's new?"

"Mother spoke to you?"

"She did." He hadn't stood when I came in. We hadn't shaken hands. "I've been looking over your trades. You should have been paying me allowance all these years."

"So deduct it."

"No, but I will ask for my original stake. As interest, I've averaged the prime rate since 1976, plus two points." At my wince he asked, "Is that a problem?"

"No problem."

"And since I've been paying taxes on your gains—"

"I had losses, too."

"I've credited you those. But overall, I'm due a refund."

"Plus interest?"

"At the same rate, yes."

He paused, distracted by my distraction, my eyes flitting from his ambiguous face to a sharper target in the mirror behind him, a backview of his head. I had thick hair (Mother's genes; Stallses lack for nothing) so as my father tallied his cut I was nonetheless consoled, for though he had my money he would never have my hair.

He slid a computer printout across his desk. A bank check was clipped to the corner. The printout listed sales prices on the stocks and options held in the account, less commission, less margin debt and interest, less capital gains tax, less a dollar-fifty for drafting the check, which (I well remember) was in the amount of $7,866.12.

It sank in. "You dumped it all?"

"As you asked," he said. "As your mother asked."

"I didn't say sell! You could have quit-claimed the whole portfolio, as is. I mean, chisel me, call in your loan—but don't sell me out. Those stocks were mine!"

"In fact they were mine. I didn't have to give you a dime."

Well, I should have torn up the check right there, flung the bits in his face. But I'm weak on spontaneity. Throwing a punch, making a pass—possible downsides occur to me instantly, and I generally reconsider. Where I'm deliberate is where I get into trouble. I've never sinned by accident.

My hand was steady as I signed a receipt for the money. Next I signed a waiver releasing Stalls Associates from all liability in my past and future affairs, then another waiver releasing my father from same. I leaned back in my chair and felt literally high, a queasy rush that lifted me over this scene like an airship over a battlefield. On the no man's land of my father's desk lay oblongs of legal paper, each carrying our names, Father's and mine, and though I admit I imagined the papers as headstones and the names on them carved legends, it wasn't a morbid vision nor sad, for even then my viewpoint seemed many years removed. Everything felt inevitable.

He tossed something else on his desk, a ticket or a playing card, it looked to me at first. It was a small photograph. "Found this the other day," I heard him say.

Pictures of my maternal forebears are common in the homes of my relatives. From paintings and daguerreotypes dead Stallses gaze reprovingly upon once-familiar rooms peopled now with layabouts disguised in the family likeness. Despite their studied, imperious poses, the subjects of these portraits cannot hide the fact they have died. It plays on their faces like distraction, like a secret on the face of a child. The picture in my hand told a similar story.

I still have it, a black-and-white passport photograph of a

man in a coarse wool suit. I know more about him now. That his baldness was premature; that his heavy brow did not falsely suggest stubbornness; that to call his expression haunted would have been as true as it was presumptuous. I know more about him now, but then, at first glance, I knew that since the picture was taken this man had died. It was there in his face, an incipient shadow. And if perhaps the photograph had simply discolored with age, the shadow was there all the same, in his face and in my father's, too, when I raised my eyes to look at him. "That man is my father," he explained. "His name was Philip Holscheimer."

"A German?"

Did he smile then? The memory changes with my mood.

"A Jew."

"You're kidding me."

"He was indeed a Jew. As am I."

"And me?"

"By blood, half."

I thought for a moment. "And no one knows—"

"But you."

"Why are you saying this now?"

"A man should know who he is."

If that was Father's purpose, to tell me who I am, the revelation worked in reverse. Part Jewish, evidently, I was born and raised a WASP. A legacy of centuries of dispersal and struggle had nothing on a short life lived under an opposite persuasion that the world was mine to lose. It was too late now to change, to turn my eyes to the past in search of clues to myself. I'd take my chances on the future. "Why have you kept it secret?" I asked.

"It wasn't a pleasant thing. In the British Army during the war, being David Holscheimer was not an advantage. So I changed my name to Halsey. I let the past—and my troubles— go. It was rather a capitulation and rather a triumph. My father took it personally, however. We never spoke again."

"Imagine that." My voice was sarcastic. His confession was a weapon, given to me. I was still clumsy in its use.

"When I left the U.K. in 1946," he continued, "it was the

16

last we saw each other. He died twenty years ago, in Palestine—Israel, I should say. My mother also died there. I learned they were dead when I tried to contact them, to tell them they had a grandson."

"Me."

"It wasn't to be. But I loved them better gone, that always had been the case. So truth was served, you see?"

I was foggy. It took a moment for me to recognize this was the perfect finish to our little play of filial woe. I folded the bank check around the photo of Father's father and put them in my pocket. My manner may have been downcast but inside I was flying, for I'd been rescued from a fate I'd always thought would get me. Something in my spirit saw redundancy everywhere. Each path looked beat to me, each aspiration lame. A drowning man on his third descent supposedly goes calmly. I'd resigned myself to going the same way. To sink, I mean, with lungs full of irony and pockets full of gold. But now—my money mine, my heritage obscured, my father transformed to a son—I was like nobody I knew. I wanted to be out of there, out of Father's office, not another word exchanged lest the blessing be revoked.

As I made to leave he said, "No reaction?"

"It's your life."

"I thought it would interest you. Your roots."

"I don't believe roots matter. Changing your name, your religion, you must not either."

"The change was cultural, mainly. And emotional."

"You chickened out."

His eyes narrowed. His hands flattened on his desk. "Sold my soul, is how my father put it."

"He must have felt humiliated."

"Certainly that. He was very proud."

"A Jew!"

"A harsh-sounding word, I've always thought."

A question occurred to me. "Would Stalls Associates have hired you as David Holscheimer?"

"In 1952? No."

"You're here as a fraud, you're saying."

"I've become what I set out to become."

Looking back, it's clear Father was working out a personal issue of little connection to me. He received my snipes graciously, as if pleased I was saying all the right lines unprompted. Throughout our exchange I'd felt on the brink of spoiling it with, say, an invitation to lunch, my treat—together we could have walked to a local deli, confessed our petty motivations and noshed on congenial foods. But I had issues of my own to work out. I'm a child of fortune, a circumstance from which it isn't so easy—because ultimately it doesn't seem worth the effort—to rise and make one's mark. Now, having been lucky enough to be victimized, I was loath to let it go. I started for the door.

"Where are you going?"

I couldn't resist: "The promised land."

"You'll be back." His assertiveness faltered. "Philip, do you think you'll be back?"

I considered but came to no answer, leaving there with my money and my grandfather's photograph in a pocket over my heart. My first impression of the photograph had held oddly true. If a playing card, the game between Father and me had ended in a draw; if a ticket, if this was theater, then the curtain fell on a question, not opening again until four years later when I returned to his office in a pinstripe suit and serious trouble. By then I was broke and being investigated; also, I was a father. I'd never seen my baby boy, didn't know his name. Still he was pure dynamite in the hands of a desperate man.

In other times, twenty-year-olds have shipped out on merchant steamers or joined the seminary, burned their draft cards or enlisted, all in a sort of enthusiastic despair that is the hallmark of intelligent youth. That's how I justify chasing profit like a madman, likewise chasing women whom I should have left alone: I was acting my age in the fashion *of* my age in hopes that I, like countless twenty-year-olds before me, might forge a past worth bragging and worth blushing about. I'm not a spontaneous person. These things must be created.

The women I'm referring to were married, though each was separated from her husband at the time I knew her. Far more disorienting than their marital states were their perfectly opposed personalities. Dating them simultaneously, I was squeezed like grease between two gears; knowing them together made Sisyphean the quesion, What do women want? One was dim and inquiring, the other bright and jaded. Sexually one did, while the other liked to get done. And spiritually their guilt derived from God looking down and the dead looking up, Catholic and Jew respectively. If women were atoms these two would have integrated instantly, forming something altogether rare while spitting me out like a waste product, an unneeded neutron, the castrato of nuclear particles.

I was living over Nick's Pizza about five blocks from my college. My room was small, smelled of pizza, and came with a garage for my old VW. (I'd sold the Buick my folks had bought me, investing the difference.) My biggest monthly expense was for leasing the Quotron terminal I kept on my kitchenette table. A lovely machine, it fed me Dow Jones news, stock and option data, bond prices, money rates, all the major indexes, and of course the market ticker.

Daily my finger was on the crucial pulse. Take the price of gold: Fears of war, fears of peace, are reflected in its fluctuation. The stock market in 1980, drifting sluggishly, told me recession was coming. When the Dow shot up in August '82, I knew the worst was over, good times lay ahead. Reagan was sure for a second term, and why not? He was perfect for the job. You want complexity, you get Nixon. You want a workaholic, you get Carter. Ford was my favorite but I was too young to vote for him.

In those days the market opened at 10 A.M. I'd phone in my buy and sell orders, then track them through the day on my Quotron. Conventional wisdom said keep your money in high-interest instruments. I went for options and speculative issues, shorting the dogs and going long on glitzy technologies. I studied newspapers and newsletters, received financial reports on cable TV and the radio. Midafternoon I'd eat a pizza, and at 4:01 I'd drink a beer as postclose announcements came in.

19

Sometimes I went out at night—to parties on campus, till it grew too strange. As a dropout I was mistrusted by my classmates. This was 1980. The high-rolling entrepreneur wasn't as exalted in collegiate circles as he would be several years later; we were still hung up on education as an end in itself. My classmates in turn seemed like children to me, complaining of "pressure," unaware of the Disneyland college really is. Time is a tailwind once you're out of school. You still don't feel it, but now, like beacons to a harbor behind you, it can be measured in landmarks slowly disappearing from view.

I ate at local restaurants, cozy eateries of a type common around expensive urban colleges. Like bars around a ballpark, these places know their clientele, which here stressed casual good taste. My first few times alone on the town I requested a second table candle to read my *Fortune* by; it seemed such a pose, I became self-conscious and couldn't digest my food. In a quiet corner I would down three courses with wine, cognac, and the Gold Card following, then I'd linger drowsily over coffee till came the time to get this body home. At home were diversions of TV and difficult novels, a little marijuana, a rented video movie; or business—strategies to plan, receipts to collate and mail to my accountant. This was my life for over two years, and I'll tell you it wasn't bad.

I didn't go to church, didn't go to temple. I mention my abstinence not to brag but to acknowledge the dilemma of having been conceived part Jew and born all WASP. I never got around to changing my name to Holscheimer. It would have been presumptuous and technically hard to pull off. I donated regularly to B'nai B'rith and appeased my heritage that way. To be a Halsey, of course, a pseudononymous fiction, I had only to be myself.

The hardest part of independent investing is coming up with new companies to consider. (I've heard of men throwing darts at the business pages, betting fortunes on the firms impaled.)

The company names blur as you scan the financial literature, and those singled out in columns and newsletters are old news by that time. You can follow your favorites and buy if they're undervalued, but there's nothing like the embryo grown, splitting three for two, to remind you you do it for love. Separated as I was from the swirl of opinion that a business office affords, I sought my leads elsewhere. A bountiful source were the published minutes of Stalls Associates' quarterly trustee meetings. Prior to our falling out, I'd received these on Father's directive. Evidently he'd neglected to scratch me off the mailing list.

Where else I got ideas a professional would laugh at: in the lobby of a branch office of a retail brokerage firm. It was laughable because such places are basically off-track betting parlors designed to serve rubes and addicts. The firms often provide in their reception lobbies, like toys in a toy store window, a Quotron and a wall-mounted ticker as enticement to customers, a contingent of whom you'll find there every workday, retirees usually, grist in the combine of institutional trading, whose talk varies inversely with the size of their portfolios, and who are never so impressed or charmed as by a fellow trader's disaster.

Now in my third year alone, I'd recently established a separate stock account expressly for impulse purchases. With $50,000 as seed money, I was day-trading entertainment stocks on the basis of movies and TV shows I'd seen the night before. I based investments on the day's weather. If sunny, I'd buy Sun Oil; if stormy, Black & Decker. And I was making money.

One morning I woke as the radio played Dylan's "Tangled Up In Blue." So at the market opening I bought a hundred IBM calls, in the money, for about $40,000. As a test, I left my apartment vowing to ignore my Quotron until the final hour of trading. But at noon I found myself outside a downtown branch office of an internationally-known stock brokerage (here nameless, pending litigation), unable to resist going in.

Opposite the receptionist's desk was an upholstered bench and a Quotron on one end table; above her head stock quotes sped right to left across a black screen, vanishing at the end like boats off the earth's edge. Three men and a woman sat together on the bench. She was punching out quotes at their command and relaying bid and ask, the men conferring, nodding, crossing their arms, deadpan disgust on their faces. The woman looked fifty, the men twenty years older—geezers all, a decrepit tribunal before which I, unshaved and ill-nourished, no doubt seemed a wandering street person or the guy who cleans the ashtrays. I felt them shift uneasily as I knelt to the Quotron, tapping "I-B-M send" on the keyboard.

The stock was down a point and three-quarters. Its size indicated a backlog of sell orders, meaning worse to come. An asterisk indicated there was recent news on the company. "IBM announced a bunch of price cuts," the woman said over my shoulder. "They're giving it away."

My option would be moving with the stock, putting me $15,000 down. I punched out the code. Make it $17,000.

The woman peered at the screen. "What month?"

"September sixties."

"Say again?" said the man beside her. He was hard of hearing, I later learned; thus loud.

"IBM options," she all but yelled. "Getting crushed!"

The old man whistled admiringly. "Big Blue. She's a hummer."

"Not today," I said.

"Gimme steel," said the second guy down, an ex-navy type with white socks and heavy black shoes. The woman tapped "X" and relayed the result. "Now Perrin," he said, and she hit "P-R-R-P."

"What company is that?" I asked her.

"Perrin Products. Hair tonic, shampoo."

"Hair *gel*," the navy guy said. "My grandson's tip."

"He works for the company?"

"He's a hairdresser. Did her."

The woman shrugged: "Let's hope he's better at stocks."

"What, Thelma, you don't like it?" He fished out his wallet and withdrew a twenty. "What'd he charge you? I feel bad."

"Keep your money, Charlie," she said. "Perrin goes up, he can make me bald."

Charlie touched his own hair, a crewcut with a waxed-up front like something bulletproof, and said to the black guy at the end of the bench, "He cuts me twice a month. I love what he does, don't you?"

"It's very attractive," the black guy said.

"This Perrin," I asked the woman. "You're all in it?"

"Oh, for a lark I am. I was going to go to Atlantic City, but I did this instead. Charlie's got some, and Mr. Wilson here. It's a takeover target supposedly. Mr. Epps at the end, he never bites. He knows better."

Just then Mr. Wilson pointed, his vision if not his hearing intact: "IBM!" I turned to see letters scoot across the ticker, off another eighth. "She's a hummer!"

I looked at the old man. "You do realize the stock is down?"

"For now. She'll roar by the close."

"What about Perrin? Like it?"

"Money down a toilet."

"It's up today on heavy volume," Charlie said defensively.

"And down tomorrow," Mr. Wilson snapped.

"If it's so bad, why do you own it?" I asked him.

"For sport, boy. A walk on the wild side. I should buy utilities and stare at them dead in the water like Epps there does all day?"

"Mr. Epps's current favorite is Avon," Thelma said of the black guy.

"For the dividend," Mr. Epps explained. He gripped a folded scrap of paper on which he'd scrawled some company names. When he saw me looking he hid it away. Stocks were real money to him, something I've never quite believed.

I stayed until the market closed. IBM teased me with a small rebound, but the specialist gave nothing back on his bid. I took it okay. Bad news to me has always held the silver lining of affirming hopelessness. My companions seemed similarly inured, for at quarter to four when Perrin Products stopped trading pending announcement, they reacted with suspicion; perhaps seeing the Depression or your children grow makes you slow to think the best. After a moment Thelma checked the news wire. "A bid's been made at nine-and-a-half." Then she smiled a little.

Charlie went "Hah!" though I think it was more for his grandson's vindication than for the money made. Thelma was thinking of Mr. Epps, who hadn't bought into the deal. "We were lucky," she apologized.

He saluted her. "You deserve it, Thelma."

Mr. Wilson looked very old. "Well, goddamn me."

"What's wrong?" Thelma asked.

"I sold yesterday."

"You didn't!"

"I did."

"But why?" Charlie said. "I told you—"

"You told me squat! Your bizarre little grandson hears a rumor and for this I risk two month's rent? I sold, all right?"

There was a long silence. Thelma said, "You took a loss?"

"Commission and a point."

Charlie slumped on the bench. "I feel bad."

More silence. "Cheer up," I said. "I have to make a phone call that's gonna cost me twenty grand." Normally you don't name dollar amounts. Talk points or volume but never points *and* volume, because there's always someone poorer who will hate you or someone richer who will sneer. I played gauche for Mr. Wilson's sake, figuring him for a man who'd appreciate another man's misfortune.

"Your IBM?" he asked.

I nodded. "She's a hummer."

They watched me walk to the receptionist's desk where I asked to use her phone. She was reluctant but I assured her it was toll free. Three minutes to four I put in my sell order at the market. In the time I signed off, thanked the receptionist and ambled back to the bench, my options were snapped up. I tapped out the code and saw the volume change an even hundred. Twenty thousand and change, by far my biggest loss to date. It was a rite of passage I'd repeat too often in the future, yet never quite as magically.

"That much for real?" Charlie asked me.

"A hundred calls. Gone."

"Gosh."

After an awkward pause they stood to leave. Mr. Wilson asked me if I needed bus fare home. I had to laugh. The others laughed, too. They were gamblers in their way, and like all gamblers they loved a loser. "I'm okay," I told him. "But thanks."

Behind me, "Sir?" rang in my ear like "Boy!" A young executive in a power tie and wide suspenders scolded me for using the office telephone. "These facilities," he said, indicating the upholstered bench where sat my elderly pals, "are for our clients' use."

"Is that so?" I'm not a total snob. Laborers and craftsmen move me to awe that is only partly condescending, but pretenders like this young V.P. compel me to regal poses. I fixed him with a fancy stare, my nose up, my voice deepening, my temperate blood suddenly combustible with its secret Semitic infusion. "Well, if you want my money, *son*, you will have to be much nicer."

He gave a dry smile. "We welcome new customers, of course."

"I'd want a break on commissions. A preferred account."

"That would require a substantial investment minimum."

"Fine. Who do I talk to?"

"Mr. Donley is very good," Thelma broke in.

The young executive said, "Mr. Donley is rather new—"

I turned to Thelma. "Take me to this wizard." She led me through the lobby to a vast back room where the brokers were kept. Their desks were paired in plexiglass booths with a rotating Quotron between them. A rumpled young man glanced up. "Hi, Ma," he said to Thelma glumly. Then he smiled and I smiled back as we recognized each other.

Timmy Donley had been three years ahead of me at college. I first met him freshman week when my roommate and I ventured giddy and scared to his room to purchase dope. He

25

didn't deal hard drugs. His style was purely pastoral, his ambition simply to keep himself forever in pot and stereo components. I'd always regarded him as the last of a breed, like priests and family farmers. It was probably un-American of me to feel sadness seeing him now, in this condition, but if ever there was someone who should have died with his headphones on, it was Timmy Donley.

He was on the telephone as I sat down. Thelma hovered until his glance dismissed her. Timmy was soothing an irate client. "I don't think we got in too high even counting those earnings revisons." He listened, nodding frantically.

"What stock?" I whispered.

"Dow," he mouthed. He held the receiver away from his face and stuck out his tongue at it.

"Tell him chemicals are cyclical."

"Chemicals are cyclical, Mr. D'Leo."

"Fertilizer, pesticide—for farmers in the spring."

This Timmy repeated.

"The stock will rise by March," I said.

"The stock will rise by March."

"Guaranteed."

"Guaranteed, Mr. D'Leo. Guaran*teed.*" Timmy grinned and gave me thumbs up. My sunk heart stirred a little in the breeze of his incompetence.

I'd already decided to throw some business Timmy's way. I wanted the company—if not Timmy Donley's, then that crew's out in the lobby. I thought some friendships might inspire me to bathe more and think better of mankind, for in my solitude I'd let things slip regarding hygiene and personal outlook.

Later, he and I had a drink at a bar. There, my marijuana Mr. Greenjeans, though fiscally retarded, proved sharp in matters of love; or shall I say love's demolition, for over our beers he came on all confessional, fully intending, I do believe now, his spilled guts to attract me like a fly. He was in love with a bank teller and wanted out of his marriage. He said, "I wish my wife would have an affair."

"To ease your guilt?"

"And possible alimony."

I told him, "Divorce these days is mostly no-fault."

"But if she had an affair she'd feel bad and grant it uncontested. I'm thinking of her, too. An affair would be good for Carrie's self-esteem. Our sex life—"

"I don't want to hear it."

"My point is, she deserves better. I'd give it my blessing." He drained his beer. "So. Philip. What's up with you?"

I had not had sex in more than two years. None. That I turned monkish in the randiest period of a man's life is today a point of pride with me. I view it as my exile in the wilderness, though my celibacy was less a bitter bout with temptation than the deliberate picking of a fight I could win. A late-bloomer, I was not highly sexed; abstinence was an undemanding path to moral superiority over my fellow citizens. Getting down with Carrie Donley made me one of the regular damned again. Still, I retain a special fondness for my period of sainthood.

As for sex with Carrie, though a pushover in her life and marriage, in bed, in mine at least, she made the rules and triumphed every time: compare fig leaves with birch rods, a veil with a push-up bra, and you will understand the two Carries that I knew. Her ideal opposite was Susan Epstein-Graulig, the woman I met later and whom I concurrently slept with. Unlike Carrie, Susan was shrewder than her husband, made more money, and had gumption enough to throw him out when her life needed improving.

But what should have been big fun (for me, the man with two girlfriends) proved unexpectedly crippling. Adapting back and forth between the two women conditioned me into perfect spinelessness. Even my fetishes and favorite perversions, which in most men are anchoring balls and chains, became in me as pliant as butter. My eventual drift into criminality was but another expression of the docility cultivated in my sexual relationships, a slippery, painless, water-soluble slide into doing what came easy.

Shortly after my chat with Timmy, his wife Carrie phoned me. He'd mentioned that he'd seen me, she said, and recalling how nice I'd been in college (when, through druggie fogs, I was fun to be around), she wanted my opinion. "Does Timmy love this bank teller?"

"He believes he does. Which counts for a lot."

"We're separated, he told you?"

"He did."

"Separated but still living together. Weird, huh?" But who am I to tell people how to part? As with sex and love, is there any real right way? She changed the subject. "Timmy says you look like a hippie."

"He looks neat and trim, and that's not a criticism."

"I look the same as ever."

As Timmy's spacy college girlfriend, Carrie was always doing needlepoint scenes from J. R. R. Tolkien on the couch in his off-campus apartment. Cocaine groupies are coiled and uppity but she was warm earth, baking hallucinogenic bread in a peasant skirt and Chinese slippers. I remembered her as curvy with heft—fine in my book, for though it sounds sexist and degrading of women, the fact is I like 'em meaty. I told her, "Timmy wants us to have an affair."

"He said that?"

"Pretty much."

"He thinks like an eighth grader. He wants me to make it easy for him, right?"

"Right."

"And the sad part is I would, if I did." She swore. "Why do I love this bum?"

"One of life's beautiful mysteries, I'm sure."

"Listen," she said. "After what you've just said, this'll sound really awful—but do you wanna have a drink sometime?"

The question seemed to bode a future of moral implication. "Why not," I said.

"You're not an eighth grader too, are you?"

"All men are eighth graders."

"Then think of me as teacher, okay? Out of bounds."

"Yes, ma'am."

We had our drink; and other drinks on other days, martinis in the afternoon and burgundy at night, grown-up drinks for grown-up assignations. Yet in three months we laid not a hand on each other, though technically we were free to. Timmy had proposed an open marriage. Problem was, as long as his affair went well, Carrie's retaliation would be unyielding devotion to her husband. Me she cast in the girlfriend role, the sympathetic eunuch, a demeaning misconstruction I blamed on her Catholicism, a religion that more explicitly than most claims virtue by default.

Everything changed when Timmy's bank teller dropped him. He got weepy about it with me at the brokerage and I gather was worse with Carrie. She felt contempt for him and for herself as well, knowing that ultimately she'd do the nice thing and forgive him. More of her private equation I won't postulate, but it added up to Carrie shedding angel wings for a frolic in the slime.

Inadvertently, we'd prepared for this turn of events, for even when it was allowed, when Timmy might have approved, Carrie and I had kept our friendship secret, tacitly holding our pristine trysts where Timmy wouldn't discover them. After his affair collapsed I felt something fresh afoot. When I picked her up one afternoon she glanced guiltily about her before climbing in my car—this was new, as was the rakish sweep of her hair and the way her several dangling earrings shone like stars you'd wish upon. "Where to?" I asked as always, but got a question back:

"Are you gay, Philip? Timmy says you're gay."

"Because I haven't slept with his wife?"

"Because in school he never saw you with a girlfriend—"

"Nothing steady, no."

"—and you don't seem to have one now. So?"

"Am I gay? Gee . . ."

"It's okay if you are. Well, not totally. It's a sickness I really do believe, but who's not a little sick, right?" Her laugh was forced and unbecoming; it made me dislike her and want to fuck her. I turned off the radio lest our particular version drown in other people's love songs.

"In fact I'm not gay. Why do you ask?"

"Because I don't wanna be disappointed."

"Ah. Okay." My heart jumped annoyingly. "Do you like pizza, Carrie?"

"Once in a while, sure. You hungry?"

"I could eat."

"You live over a place, right?"

"By coincidence."

"Good. So drive."

"Righto."

She indulged me on the way, let me circle our imminent moment with juvenile innuendo. I was never a womanizer. My sexual strategies were formed in prep school and based on guerrilla codes, meaning girls must be laid in such a way they will not know it's happened. So as I drove I cracked jokes about oyster pizzas and the possible proclivities of my Greek landlords (two brothers owned my building, a Mediterranean Mutt and Jeff) all the while fretting secretly about which side I'd end up lying on—with Carrie in foreplay, to be absolutely clinical. Because I'm righthanded, and to keep my right hand free I must lie on my left side, my left hand being clumsy as a hambone, barely able to open a car door much less anything as complicated as a woman's jeans or labia. I needn't have worried, though. Rather than on my right or left side, I spent most of that evening on my back. Carrie was looking to conquer something, and I was game to go down.

Inside my door she asked if I had herpes. I explained that I'd been safely out of circulation, and she rewarded me with a kiss. She stepped back and took off her clothes, then she stepped forward and hugged me. "Now lick my teeth." I didn't hesitate. Her teeth were smooth and mostly white and their flavor kind of grew on me.

Streetlights ignited outside. Below my bedside window a red neon pizza sign cast an ember glow across the ceiling and across Carrie's shoulders and breasts. Gazing up at her, at her fiery skin, I remember thinking the city is burning and I don't even care. My apartment had that insular feel of maybe the world could end in flames and I wouldn't know for months; it compared to a beauty salon or a monastic cell, places where time stands still, where all energy and thought are focused past the everyday toward some ultimate future: a cocktail party, God's face, or, in my case, my emergence as a multimillionaire after years of heroic exile. A recurrent daydream of mine is to survive some sort of hideous trial, a kidnapping, a mugging, a terrorist assault, that afterward would imbue my soul and blankest stare with automatic depth. But if I fancied life alone to be that trial, here I was with Carrie, flunking. Because I was definitely enjoying her company. Her ripply round weight rose and collapsed around my pelvis like a balloon filled with warm soft cement. She'd given me her thumb to suck with instructions to say please. This embarrassed and stimulated me, as the Victorian pornographers used to say, unto the point of crisis. My hands were upraised like somebody surrendering or signalling touchdown. As she ground her hips into orgasm, I tugged her nipples and bit her thumb so that her feelings too would be mixed.

Later I asked where things stood with Timmy now that his mistress had dumped him. "He wants to be my hubby again. I wanna stay separated. For a while." Forever is always scary. For a while should be fun—but as spoken by Carrie it sounded like prison time, a sentence served as punishment. I resented, after what had been the best sex of my life, being so unappreciated.

"I'm separated too, you know."

"From your family, you mean?"

"Yes," I said, voice whiney with hurt that I didn't imagine was genuine, "from my family." Omitting the Jewish part, I'd told her how my father, over money, had cut my family connections like an angry playmate taking home his toys.

"So we're both alone," she whispered. "No one knows we're here."

"That's right. This hole in the wall, this bed, this moment in time—no one alive knows we're here. I like it, actually."

"I hate it."

31

"Why? *We* know we're here. You and me—"

"And God."

"Him, too." A mistake. Carrie's body tensed. "Come on. I thought women were better at this."

"Better at what?"

I was careful: "At illicit companionship."

"Adultery, Philip. A mortal sin."

"Timmy did it first. An eye for an eye."

"That's stupid. And that's not why I'm here. I'm here for me, not him."

I nuzzled her in gratitude for what seemed a compliment. "Forget this God stuff. He forgets us, after all."

"I don't believe that. I believe we're watched and judged by a demanding God."

"Humbug."

"I can't talk to you."

"Who needs talk when we have this?" But in her pique she'd turned on me the pale wall of her back.

Our postcoital theosophy had aroused some unexpected pangs in me. From the bedside table I withdrew the old photograph of my grandfather that Father gave me at our last meeting, three years earlier. At that moment it seemed the man in the picture was more than my grandfather, more than a gray-visaged ghost named Philip Holscheimer. He was, in the apparent stern probity of what little I knew about him, a lofty saint of principle who'd disowned his son for reasons bigger than love, and who probably would have disowned me, too, for lying in this bed, with this woman, feeling this good.

I hadn't looked at the picture for quite a long time. Somehow in the interim it had become a spooky relic, a gothic icon to stir my fear and channel me toward moral improvement. The picture's power lay in its mystery, in all it didn't say. To thwart the mystery I now filled in the details for Carrie—of who the man was and what sort of people he came from, and what he'd done to my father. "He banished your dad because your dad changed his name? Wow." I angled the photo to the neon-lighted window. My grandfather's face went red, his pewter-colored pupils darkening. It scared me. I touched

Carrie's shoulder in a reflex of seeking rescue. She covered my hand, kissed me, turned her face away. I realized she was confronting her own inquisitors. I realized she wanted to leave. She said, "I gotta say, Philip. Your grandfather is the kind of man who disgusts me."

"He's dead, in case you're worried you'll meet him."

"Good."

"Carrie!"

"He was a shitty parent."

"He had his values and didn't bend them. There's something admirable in that."

"A parent should be a sap for their kid first and admirable second. A child depends on that, and deserves it. No wonder your dad is so messed up."

"My father is a lost, cowardly man. With no excuse for it."

"My mom's hardcore Catholic and still the crazy things I've done I can always tell her and she'll always try to understand. She's true to me because I'm her child. I can tell her anything."

"Gonna tell her about us?" A cruel question. I crept to her ear. "Forgive me. I like you."

"You make me feel crummy."

"Feel good. God loves you."

"Hah."

"He's your parent, isn't he? Doesn't the Bible say God forgives everything?"

She turned to face me. "You should teach Sunday school."

I nuzzled my groin into hers, sliding under her like a baby under a blanket. "I like you as teacher better."

Which made her smile. As she pinned my wrists against the mattress her smile turned to a leer. "I dunno, kid. You bring out some sorta devil in me."

She lowered her breasts to me like a volunteer offloading care packages. "It's a gift," I sighed. I was twenty-two. She was twenty-five. We knew nothing, is my point.

Our affair, Carrie's and mine, put her husband through some classic changes. Timmy knew she was seeing someone, and he bent my ear at the brokerage wondering who it was. With his wife he was lost. Had he ranted and raved, hit her, she would only have found it easier to keep on hurting him; and pathetic displays generally provoke contempt before remorse. But open marriage had been his idea. Blaming himself for his dilemma, it was himself he tried to change. He jogged, weightlifted, resumed potsmoking and religion—together, that is, getting high then going to Mass, so the effects were canceled out.

Carrie meanwhile blossomed. Laying Timmy waste fulfilled her somehow, graced her like a flattering scar. Her wit grew sharp and quick and dark. Her appetites grew—for sex and food and culture—while her talk of God and mother dropped almost to nil. Her occasional guilt pangs were ennobling and necessary to her growth from bimbo to queen, for there is no greatness without guilt, no depth without a bottom. One day I spied her staring at herself in a mirror with the implacable chill of a goddess sculpted in marble. "Timmy's hurting pretty bad," she said, partly to me and partly to her own reflection. Then she shrugged, "It has to be." Impressive.

I felt a little bad myself, and tried to make amends by making Timmy money. I spent many gratis hours compiling stock recommendations for his clients' portfolios. I moved more of my outside funds into my account at Timmy's brokerage to put extra commissions in his pocket. The way he moped around, he hardly noticed all I did for him. The guy was sinking fast and his mother was concerned.

"It's his wife," Thelma said one day. Everyone was there on the bench in the brokerage lobby. "She's gotten too big for her britches."

"Which were big before," Mr. Wilson cackled.

"He should throw her out," Charlie said. "That's what my wife did to me."

"Except he loves her," Mr. Epps said.

Thelma said, "Carrie's dragging him down just when he's finding himself. My Timmy's getting noticed, you know. I heard his boss talking. Timmy should divorce her—start fresh, buy a condominium. He needs a tax deduction with all the money he's making. You should have one, too," she told me. As my account manager's mother, she knew my business too well.

"Buy a house," Charlie suggested. "You can deduct the taxes and mortgage interest."

"I'd prefer something more speculative. A couple of housing lots, maybe."

"You can't depreciate land," Mr. Wilson said. "Get some commercial property. My brother owns a filling station, pays not a dime to the government."

"Where they're developing Washington Boulevard is where I would buy," Mr. Epps said. "Near the university in the old Greek section. They're fixing it up real nice."

"It's gentrification," Thelma argued. "They're driving out the poor Greeks."

"It can't be helped," Mr. Wilson said, and Mr. Epps agreed: "It's dog-eat-dog, I'm afraid."

"Cat-eat-mouse," Charlie nodded. "Shark-eat-fish."

"Well, I think it's tragic," Thelma said, "and immoral." Then to me: "Hit Raytheon, dear. They're bidding on a missile guidance system."

I punched the Quotron code. "Up two points."

"Bull's-eye," she smiled.

The area they were talking about, Washington Boulevard, was where I lived. And while I'd noticed the new development, it hadn't dawned on me to participate. My bracket and my short-term gains were killing me taxwise, however, and real estate with its paper losses was a logical next step.

I phoned a local realty office. The agent I spoke to was named Ms. Epstein-Graulig. She impressed me with her savvy and with the way her voice glazed over when we started discussing her commission; refreshingly (after Timmy and Carrie), she knew what she was worth. Before our meeting I got a haircut, shaved, broke an old suit out of mothballs. Real estate intimidated me, likewise white collar women. My earring I kept another day before that too was scrapped.

At her office she introduced herself as Susan. She was a compact, sharp-dressed woman around thirty. Her pinned-back dark hair followed from the planes of her cheekbones like the sides of a ship's hull following from the prow; my impression was of someone leaning into life, into a headwind created of forward motion, a resistance efficiently cleaved. Her nose, she later told me, had been fixed, and her lips with their hunting-bow curl proved adept at delivering barbs. You could say about Susan that if she had a child who closely resembled her, it would be better off a boy. Her face (when I knew it; I can't speak for the nose) was a fortunate harmony of potentially clashing parts. Alter the mix even slightly, and you'd get a girl with an uphill battle against unfair first impressions, seeming perhaps ratlike whereas her male twin might seem elfin; men have more room for error in these things. I make the point because Susan eventually did have a child. Mine. To this day I've never seen him, but I'm told he's a dead ringer for his mom. Better, then, that he's a boy, for Susan's particular beauty would be hard to duplicate. We want our children to have every advantage, more so when they can't have us.

We chatted briefly in her office. I told her my needs, my price range. With a selection of listings in hand, we toured the area in her car. Our tour was enlightening to say the least. On occasion I've sat down with friends who knew nothing about the stock market, who dismissed it as grubby and arcane, and I've elicited from them the reflex envy that even rich kids feel upon learning they could be richer. Regarding real estate I was the uninformed skeptic. It seemed too tangible to me, like sweaty coins and wadded dollar bills; I prefer my money computerized. But Susan made a believer of me, explaining how real estate's loopholes and capital growth are treasures in the grime.

We drove by a string of retail stores that Susan explained was an investor's dream. Rents covered taxes, mortgage interest, and maintenance costs; and, in those days before the tax-reform bill of Reagan's second term, accelerated depreciation could create a loss on paper applicable to other income—and money saved is money earned. "My boss owns that property,"

Susan said of one place. "Neil Gray, Gray Realtors. He's also my father-in-law."

"If he's Neil *Gray*, how did 'Epstein-Graulig' come about?"

"Epstein's my maiden name. My husband, Neil's son, changed his name from Gray to Graulig. A Jewish roots thing."

"My father went the other way. I should have been someone named Philip Holscheimer. But I was raised, you know—"

"A goy. It's no crime."

"Oh? Sometimes I feel robbed. Not of being Jewish. I mean, how much can I care, never having been? But things do feel pretty arbitrary to me, generally."

"Things *are* arbitrary," she said with a sudden vehemence that took me aback. "Everyone has to learn that eventually."

Her implication was that I hadn't learned it yet. My cover was blown, I thought. No executive here, just a kid with cash. I wilted in my suit.

She pulled the car to the curb and pointed out my window. "For you." I was surprised to see we were in front of my pizza-parlor home. The building was for sale, she said. In fact there were quirks to the deal that made it ideal for a man like me (her words). Youth, apparently, could stand the little ugliness the purchase would involve. The building was owned by two brothers, Frank and Nick Bakes. (I knew this; they were my landlords.) Frank had controlling interest and now was dissolving the partnership to force sale of the building. "His wife ran off with Nick," Susan said.

I hadn't seen Frank around for weeks. His brother Nick, who owned the pizza business downstairs, had indeed, come to think of it, lately borne the gallows look of a man messed up in love. "Is this pertinent?" I asked.

"You want background or not?"

"Yes, ma'am," I said, instantly adopting the good-boy persona Carrie's sexual tastes had schooled into me.

"Well, Frank is on a vendetta and wants out of the property at any price. Meet him, and in five minutes you'll get the whole sorry saga about his faithless wife and brother, tears and all. It's pathetic the way these macho men revert."

"Such is love." Again her response jolted me:

"People in love should *want* to leave their lovers! Staying should be an option weighed against other options of independence and selfishness, a choice made new, from the heart, every day." Her eyes blazed; there could be no argument to this theory clearly dear to her. "Clinging kills a relationship!"

"You've had experience in the matter?"

"You could say that," with an off-key laugh. At her evident frazzlement my confidence gained:

"With your husband?"

"My soon-to-be ex. We're separated now."

"And the separation was your idea?" This was forward of me. But after two years of chastity, my afternoons with Carrie had crowned me king of love. It seemed my privilege to presume.

She nodded. "I'm the bad guy, yes."

"I'm separated, too."

"How long were you married?"

"I wasn't married, exactly. It was a different kind of thing."

"I see." She gave a twinkly look that threw me. Warily, I changed the subject:

"So how come your father-in-law hasn't fired you? Wouldn't that be the least he could do for his son?"

"Well, Neil—Mr. Gray, my boss—he prefers me to Gershom. My husband."

"Prefers you to his own son?"

"Yes. To be frank."

"How nice for—Gershom, did you say?"

"Changed from Gerald. *Hebraized*, same as Graulig from Gray. And Gershom's doing fine, believe me. He has a martyr need which is being incredibly stroked by all this. Between him and his father I'm the battlefield. They've been warring for years."

"Boys and their dads."

"Exactly. Girls with their mothers, we want equality, equal time—that's fair at least. Men don't want fair, they don't want a middle ground. They have to look up or down. They have to take it or dish it out."

I thought a moment. "It's possible."

"My husband," she continued, the subject still raw, "quit law school, which he actually liked, for urban sociology—big money there, let me tell you. Then he pulls the name change. Now he's studying Talmud, Hebrew, keeps kosher. He created this whole left-wing, pseudo-rabbinical identity just to bug his father!"

"Did it work?"

"Did it work! Neil's a Republican, a self-made millionaire. Loves spending money, loves Israel, dislikes Jewy Jews. He's the total opposite of Gershom. Gershom likes old things. His father likes—" She groped for a word.

"Young things?"

Susan smiled. "Very good. Neil's been a widower for years, but he just got remarried. To Dominique."

"Not exactly Old Testament."

"She's pure Viking. It put Gershom over the edge."

"It's hardly his business."

"He can't help it. He says Dominique's a closet Nazi and a gold digger, too. He insisted they have a prenuptial agreement to protect Neil's assets. But Neil's a romantic. He said no way."

"Gershom has his greedy side. I like him better."

"He's thinking of our children, he says."

"Oh. You have kids."

She shook her head. "It's a vain wish, at this point. Yet he hopes."

"Even now?"

"We haven't been separated very long."

"Since yesterday, right?" This was a joke. Not funny:

"How'd you guess?"

"You split up yesterday!"

"He moved his stuff out last night, yeah."

I almost laughed. "That explains a lot."

"Explains what?" In answer, I tapped two fingers together in imitation of flapping jaws. Her face colored. "God, you're right. I'm sorry. I'm usually much sharper." She proceeded to prove it: Her eyes that had faltered in embarrassment at my remark fixed on me coldly, her tone bright as a new straight razor. "It's just that you're such a good listener, Philip. Gay guys have that gift, I know. I have a gay friend, and he and I share everything. He's so accepting, so wise. I should introduce you."

I should have laughed off this lame attack. But believing her to be sincere, I responded sincerely, an unformed young man cut where it counts by a recurring misconception. "I am not gay! I have no particular prejudice against homosexuality, still it's important to me that not every bitch I meet thinks I'm queer! What possible thing about me gives you that impression?"

"Guess I hit a nerve. Well, there's what you said about being separated but not married. And there's the earring."

"The earring! Don't you know the earring is hip? The earring says I'm unfettered by bourgeois poses and aspirations. Everybody wears an earring!"

"To me it says you're a trust fund rebel who lives in the suburbs somewhere, a lawnmowing man." She was laughing now.

"But straight," I insisted.

"But straight."

"Damn right." A moment passed. "Actually," I said, pointing out the car window, "I live here. Upstairs. Alone."

"You're the other tenant? We knew about the woman."

"Mrs. Bakes. She's my neighbor."

"She's history. Her lease is up and there's no renewal option. We did a best-use study of the property and what's indicated upstairs is medical offices. Unless she's a doctor," Susan said, "she's got to vacate. We had no record of the second upstairs tenant, of you. We assumed the lease had been lost."

"I never had a lease. I'm renting month to month. No chains, get it? Listen," I proposed, "we're here, we've got a parking spot—let's have a pizza."

"Bad idea. Nick Bakes is probably inside. He knows I'm trying to sell the building."

"So?"

"The ground floor is zoned for retail, but a pizza joint is not desirable. I see a boutique here, something upscale."

"He must have a lease."

"Nope. He and his brother own the building as Bakes Partners. Nick rents from the partnership. There was a lease once, but they never bothered to renew since it's all been buddy-buddy, till now. Now Frank wants blood. See, without a lease, Nick loses double. He can't keep his business here, but he can't sell it either because without a lease he's got nothing to sell. Everything he's worked for will be lost. Nick's screwed, basically."

"For love."

She shrugged. "If he sees me, he'll think I'm involved."

"Which of course you're not."

"Don't get holy with me! If the deal's too sticky for you, fine. Someone else can buy the building. Someone else will."

"I don't know, bumping tenants and all."

"Your lawyer does it, not you. And the negative stuff's only temporary. There are positive aspects I haven't even mentioned."

"Go on."

It had grown warm in the car. With a squirm she removed her jacket, releasing perfume smells and unveiling a barely undulant vista of cream silk blouse. She was flat-chested and thus Carrie Donley's physical opposite—that distinction alone aroused me. Of the hormone disturbances caused by lust, the main one is presumption. The more you lust the more you presume, until at last the girl has no say at all: You will fuck her and she will love it. This dilation of ego and blood vessels climaxes, for men, in constriction; for women (I gather), in a powerful blooming, like a flower fed too much plant food. I underwent such a process in Susan's car. My face warmed when she removed her jacket, my self-approval soared. Yet as if in spasm, my throat clenched all too quickly and my eyelids squeezed shut in pleasurable shame. I seemed to have ravished her in my mind and already was on to regretting it. Glancing up from redoing a button, Susan smiled, pleased to think she knew my thoughts. To conceal my embarrassment I too squirmed out of my coat. She helped with one sleeve, and if worsted wool were human skin I would have needed a towel right there, to mop up. My knotted stomach growled.

"Was that you?" she said.

"I'm a pig, I know."

Her laugh was motherly. "We'll take a tour, then we'll eat. Somewhere else."

Our coats on our arms, we walked around the building. Two floors, a flat roof, three thousand square feet—a nice starter project, she called it. The advantage, she said, was that most of the groundwork for upgrading the property had been completed. Technical drawings, planning and zoning approval—all secured and paid for. She bid me imagine the white-painted brick sandblasted back to red, the light fixtures replaced with brass sconces, the alley and rear parking lot resurfaced and edged with plantings. She said the garages in back would be razed to expand the lot. As the garages abutted a steep earth embankment, this seemed a costly improvement.

"For offices you need the added parking. If you're gonna be cheap about it you're wasting my time and yours. You gotta spend money to make money." Her tone pissed me off. I felt like buying the building just to show her who's boss.

Cast-iron stairs led to a balcony outside the upstairs apartments, the apartment doors side by side, a never-used ten-speed next to mine. Susan bounded up the stairs without touching the rusted railing. "Let's inspect the Bakes place."

"We can't do that!"

"I have a key."

"What if she's home?"

"What if she is? I haven't been inside. I should know what I'm selling." Her knock was answered as I reached the balcony. She handed her business card to the old woman. "Susan Epstein-Graulig, Gray Realtors. May we come in?"

"Yes?" the woman said with a heavy accent. She wore a black dress, black stockings, lavender slippers. Seeing me she smiled, "Hi, Philly."

"Hello, Mrs. Bakes. How are you?"

"Okay. You need metches?"

"No, no matches today. We're here—why are we here, Susan?"

"To inspect the apartment. As you asked."

"Right." In the past, Mrs. Bakes had received me only as far as her doorway. Her kitchen, I saw now, was bigger than my whole place, with curtains and matching wallpaper, a spotless stove, a pitcher of cut flowers. Peering into the living room, where Susan already was, I saw slipcovered furniture and a plastic sheet running over the carpet. The bedrooms were to the left, the apartment in an L-shape around my corner studio. "Nice place," I said to Mrs. Bakes. It amazed and shamed me; except for my files and Quotron machine carefully arranged on my kitchenette table, my apartment was a fanciful version of Calcuttan squalor, as I thought befitted anyone forced to make a home on a noisy city boulevard above a pizza parlor.

The old woman smiled, waiting. "Thenk you."

Susan returned to the kitchen. "Two full baths," she noted.

"One is shower," Mrs. Bakes said. "I no use."

"That'll help your renovation costs," Susan told me. "For medical offices, you need extra plumbing." She asked Mrs. Bakes, "The pipes are good?"

"Nikos, he fix. What is medical?"

"I saw Nick's picture on your bureau. Frank's, too. I'm sorry about the trouble in your family."

Mrs. Bakes gazed upward prayerfully. "Is bad for Frank. He is confuse very much. The wife she is a tramp. Nikos will learn."

"It's always the woman," Susan muttered harshly.

"What is medical?" the woman asked again.

"Perhaps we should go," I said to Susan.

"She ought to be told. The building's converting to medical offices, Mrs. Bakes. Apartment leases will not be renewed."

"My son Frank say I can stay always."

"Frank is selling. He'll have no power to help you."

"You buy?"

"I'm the broker."

"You buy, Philly? For medical?" Mrs. Bakes gripped Susan's business card like a dreaded telegram. Before I could answer, the woman began pushing us out the door. "Please to go, you and you. I call Frank now. He say I can stay, okay?"

But Susan wouldn't quit:

"Make plans, I'm telling you. Find a new place." As the door swung shut she plucked her card from Mrs. Bakes's hand and snapped it in her purse.

"Why did you do that?" I asked her.

"To keep anonymous. These Greeks are hotheads."

"The other, I'm talking about. Why did you torture her?"

"I did her a favor. The sooner she accepts the inevitable, the better for her. There's no alternative."

"You can't say that. She may talk to Frank, convince him not to sell. She may heal the rift with his brother, you don't know."

"Sure, coddle the boys and blame the tramp. It's always the same with these old-country biddies, these mountain peasants—they hate women!"

"I hope Frank lets her stay. I hope he doesn't sell."

"You don't understand. The building's already been sold."

"Then why did you bring me here?"

"Because the new owner wants to turn it over. Immediately."

"For a quick profit."

"Not at all. He's hoping to break even at best."

"Why is he selling, then?"

"Because of Nick Bakes," Susan said. "And because of Mrs. Bakes—and because of you, when he thought you might be poor and feeble. As the new owner he doesn't want to do what is required to make money with this property: throw them out. I'm talking about Neil Gray, my boss."

"Your father-in-law has bought the building?"

She nodded. "They've gone to contract, him and Frank. Now Neil's having second thoughts. But he's already put ten percent down, and if he breaks the deal, he'll lose the down payment. So he's decided to buy the property and sell it right away, as is. To make the deal more attractive, he'll cut the commission to three percent instead of six. Which means I'll get paid but the company won't."

"That's the bait?"

"That and the price, which is super-low. Plus, as I said, most of the prep work's been done."

"Less the matter of evicting an old foreign lady and her lovestruck son."

"You're in the right legally. But granted, it'll take some balls."

"Chutzpah."

"If you like."

"Which Neil lacks? Why do I doubt that?"

"My husband's been working on him, calling him slumlord. Neil's selling the place to prove him wrong. Dominique's none too thrilled about it. She realizes it's a guaranteed moneymaker."

"I feel I know these people."

She smiled. "You're funny."

"You're pretty."

"My. Thank you."

"You're welcome."

A pause. "Well?"

"Well what?" Play dumb, I thought. It worked with Carrie.

"You want it?"

This seemed crude. "Who wouldn't?" I said uncertainly.

She took a step forward. Terrified to look down, I sensed that she was more bosomy than I'd first thought, judging from the tension of air compressed between us. "We'll start right away."

"Gee," I retreated, "I was hoping we could eat first."

After a heartbeat's hesitation, her eyes narrowed but her smile surprisingly broadened, gathering power like a bear trap being pried open. My monkey grin ached on my face. "You little punk," she said, not unkindly, and jabbed my chest with her long-nailed forefinger. She clanged down the iron stairs, laughing over her shoulder, "I never come second, Mr. Halsey. Least of all to lunch!"

Sorry for offending her, I gave chase, even offered to buy the stupid building. "We'll call it square, okay?" She hopped in her car and screeched away in a seemingly permanent gesture.

But when I went to Gray Realtors the next day (no earring), I found a contract prepared with my name at the bottom, awaiting my signature and a one-percent binder. Susan tilted her chair and eyed me triumphantly. I felt naked before her. The feeling made me desire her more, for there is something behind ironic postures that loves to be debunked. Any pretense of roguishness thoroughly trashed, I preened in mute expectancy before this pushy female. Like a fawn on wobbly legs I awaited her, my vigilant doe, to nuzzle up and nurse me.

But Susan didn't want to mother. On the contrary, she was, in a phrase, looking for daddy. Which leads me to the following theorem: If you're going to abase yourself with someone, it helps to despise them a little. My buying the building merely to save face gave Susan the cause for contempt she needed, the confidence to relax, unbutton, uncoil. Then there was the cruelty aspect. Once I signed the purchase agreement, I set about evicting Mrs. Bakes and Nick's Pizza with impressive resolution. Emotional ardor is so easily faked these days, certain proofs have arisen by which we confirm what people feel about us, proofs ranging from valentines to suicide; and childish as these are, who isn't someway touched by them? Susan was touched, for in a world of hollow gestures, here was I, through eviction proceedings, ready and willing to hurt people who didn't deserve it. My combination of naiveté and meanness appealed to her. We take poets to bed in the hope they'll turn savage, in a poetic sort of way.

A few weeks later, Susan asked me to bind her wrists and spank her. The next day I asked Carrie to spank me. Life is a journey.

Before that summer of '83, I'd mixed business and pleasure like ingredients of a cocktail; sipped daily yet in moderation, the mixture kept me mildly buzzed, kept me interesting to myself. The added dose of Susan and my real estate endeavor jostled my equilibrium. The puritan in me imposed recovery measures. When I ran out of marijuana one day I didn't resupply. Six-packs remained unopened in my refrigerator for weeks. An awareness of clutter set me to cleaning my room. But truly it was my head becoming cluttered, a mist becoming fog, so with a willful tilt of mind I plunged full speed ahead.

As in a maze of mirrors, things reflected other things too

perversely to believe. At the brokerage I watched Timmy and my money, but saw Carrie and my building; with Susan, I dwelled as much on business matters as on master/maid sex dramatics. And always one woman reflected the other, myself the lens between them, the transparency through which their images were inverted. I kept them in the dark about each other, though having made no promises there were no promises to break. (I did promise to stay free of disease. Carrie feared herpes. Susan was the first person I ever heard mention AIDS in connection with herself and not only with some afflicted minority. I assumed her comment was another gay gibe aimed at me, but she was thinking presciently of heterosexual carriers. For their part, the women promised not to get pregnant. The Boy Scout motto or the Seventh Commandment is the moral here.)

Within a maze of mirrors, smudges tell where not to go. I was Carrie and Susan's smudge, and Peter Rice was mine. Peter was the executive who'd scolded me for using the receptionist's phone my first afternoon at the brokerage. He managed office operations and several preferred accounts. I'd much disliked him that first day. My opinion had since modified: still a turd, but smart.

The secretaries called him Peter in a manner I thought unseemly. When he spoke to the oldsters and me in the lobby, he dispensed his wisdom like bread crumbs. In time, however, he took deferring tones with me. "As Mr. Halsey could tell you," he'd say to a new broker. Or, "As Phil here well knows . . ." I liked it. My investment success had never translated to fancy clothes and foreign cars, my street act calling for Salvation Army style. But someone else waving my flag was fine. I was good at what I did. Effort and knack had come together in a facsimile of ease, of luck sustained three years running and netting out, before the building and Peter Rice, at $400,000 plus. Beyond my own account I was now managing Timmy's as well, holding his hand through various moves while he sang the cuckold blues. His superiors had given him a raise. Where was my reward?

Peter knew I'd been helping Timmy. Several times he'd noted how Timmy's turnaround coincided with my arrival.

"You must be good luck," he winked. He was stroking me, and some weeks before I bought the building he proffered his first carrot. We were pissing side by side in the men's room. "Tomorrow," he said to the tile wall, "Bradley-Burke will offer thirty-five a share for Cleary Brothers." And as he zipped up: "You're welcome."

Remember the year: 1983. The market, mildly bullish, was nowhere near the boomtown mode of 1986. The recession was just passing; recovery brought more talk of interest rate relief than of corporate acquisitions. Acquisitions happened, of course. Stocks soared, fortunes multiplied on the swell of rumors and tips. Rumors and tips they remained, however, not yet the pejorative "inside information" they would become later. More than a description, a crime needs a criminal, a major malefactor to clarify, by example, extremes of bad behavior. Deceit has Judas, the worst has Hitler, greed now has Michael Milken—but not in '83. I lacked a role model, you could say.

I'd heard tips like Peter's before, and chasing them had never paid off. So I was plenty amazed when, after the next day's close, it came over the wire that Bradley-Burke indeed had bid thirty-five dollars per share for Cleary. Cleary's stock was up four points on takeover rumors; its options likewise had jumped and likely would triple tomorrow, as the arbitrageurs moved in. But for most investors the game already was closed. When Peter and I met again, he asked how well I'd done. I told him I hadn't bothered.

"For shame." His grin was the hood ornament on his British sports-car face. Too, there was a trace of Britain in his speech, a congenital affectation. I learned later that Peter was the scion of Manhattan money so old it had grown envious and petty, young again, rejuvenated by the effrontery of immigrant wealth and vitality. "You may get another shot," he told me.

I shrugged indifferently, but found myself hoping I would.

In the parking lot a few days later he murmured in my ear, "Ellard and Technograf."

"Ellard bid what, sixty? That's old news."

"The deal is *off*. The announcement comes Thursday."

"How do you know?"

"The better question is, why am I telling you?" Again the smile as he answered the question: "We took an instant dislike to each other. It's the classic start of a fine relationship."

"I don't want a relationship with you."

"Business, kid! A golden goose. But it takes two." Carrie called me kid when we were in bed sometimes. The benefits of letting her outweighed the brief belittlement, which was my rationale for letting Peter, too. "T-graf puts should fly," he explained. "They trade on the Pacific exchange."

"I know where they trade."

"Then snap to it. This news is hundred proof."

"Peter," I said, not to be bullied, "you should know that I still dislike you."

"But do you love me?"

"I beg your pardon?" He was out of my league, I concede now.

"Because you're going to love me, Philip. Love and adore."

I acted on his tip. As a gimmick of autonomy, however, I changed the play somewhat. Rather than short Technograf I went long on Ellard Systems. Industry analysts considered Ellard's bid for Technograf too high—the deal falling through would cause its stock to rise. Wednesday I bought near-term calls for $10,000. On news of no deal, the stock ticked up and my options followed. Friday at the open I sold for $14,000. Then I checked Technograf. The stock had been trading around 56. The announcement sent it plummeting, nine points by midafternoon when traders covering their calls bought in to staunch the bloodflow. Ten grand worth of puts at 50 would have made me a hundred grand minimum. I'd hooked myself, is what I'd done. A hundred grand had got away and left me feeling teased and cheapened. Even for dealing with Peter Rice, $100,000 was respectable; $4,000 was an insult. I was torn. I wanted another try at a jackpot but I dreaded his collusion. Not for moral reasons; it was the man himself, his flirty way with money and me. I decided to stand pat. Do nothing; react. Then I met Susan Epstein-Graulig and bought her building. After that, it didn't take long for me to see I should make love to Peter Rice, figuratively speaking.

In many ways my real estate move was timely. To raise cash for the purchase, I got out near my highs on Damon and Diebold. The prime rate had dipped to ten-and-a-half, so mortgage rates were relatively reasonable. I required a portfolio yield of thirteen percent annually to carry the empty building, and, since I needed to vacate my old place, to support myself in a new apartment. Maintaining such a performance wouldn't be easy, though I'd bettered that over three years of recession. Of course I'd pay no income tax, and once the building was online I'd collect $7,000 a month in rents. The difficulty was getting the property refurbished and occupied fast. Susan said no problem.

She was, this woman who in private did anything I said, arrogant in commercial matters and imperious in public. To the world we were broker and client. In restaurants together I would no more have held her hand or licked her fork as dipped my wick in flambé. Discretion ruled; intimacy naturally suffered. Never again did we speak as candidly as that first time in her car, except about money. Money was our bond, the giddy, mischievous referent that sex must be when lovers also are friends.

Beyond broker and client, there was a bit of the trainer and performing seal in our relationship. Regarding the building, she had all the answers and I had all the risk. In the days before we closed the sale, a pattern developed of my appearing at her office wretched with anxieties of all that could go wrong. I'd heard rumors of a tenant's market, a surplus of office space; foreclosure haunted my dreams like a spider. On to other deals by now, Susan uttered bitchy asides to her colleagues of my intrusion in her workday.

It was almost scripted. I would show up mornings, her colleagues would trill, "He's ba-ack," and Susan, looking put upon, would ask, "What now?" I'd confess my latest fear— sleazy contractors, say—only to be put off: "Could you get me a decaf, Phil? And a Sweet'n Low light for Alison." The trick performed, I'd get a treat: "Relax. When the bids come in, we'll take the middle one. No crooks or fly-by-nights. For a Richie Rich, Phil, money really spooks you."

"A Richie Rich?" Titters behind me—from Alison and the other brokers, and Lyle the secretary.

"Excuse me. A market speculator," Susan amended, telling them winkingly, "He *is* a stockmarket whiz, you know."

I said to her, "You could use help in that department. Your money's where, a savings account?"

"In my car, in furniture, and investment clothes."

"Spent, in other words."

She laughed. "Isn't he funny, Alison?"

Eventually I got so well trained I brought coffee to the office unasked. (Alison came to expect it, even phoned me one morning to ask what's the holdup.) I feared disappointing Susan in any way. She'd found me a real estate attorney and attended our first meeting, interviewed contractors and took their bids while I sat by looking mysterious. My dependency made a queen of her, which I resented. She wanted me to resent it, wanted me, when alone with her, to claim punitive tributes of my own. Then I was king and she was subject—or trainer and seal if you like, me the trainer and she one the who tumbled and barked on command. Embarrassing stuff, these bedroom requitals. It made for sexy sex and doomed attachment, but we weren't ones to quibble.

As a man in the middle I was sensitive to changes in the women flanking me. Carrie, for one, had become strikingly sharp-tongued, a shift that had its parallel in her developing sexual dominance. No longer limited to dirty talk, now we did the things she'd once only whispered in my ear, played them out with paddles and handcuffs and mail-order implements of ingenious utility and eye-opening anatomical realism. And just as Susan felt compelled to even out our sexual scorecard by insulting me in public, so did I with Carrie. Carrie's job at a bakery, her vocabulary, her fair-weather Catholic faith, were all prey to my needling. Finally she ordered, "Just you fucking stop!" I obeyed at once.

Logic suggested that my relationship with Susan would follow a parallel dynamic, that her public treatment of me would begin to reflect the softer submissive side she'd revealed in private. But no. Her sexuality proved more grudging than Carrie's joyous play-acting. Susan continued to seek redress for our intrusive intimacies through her sternly maintained distance and sarcasm. It never occurred to me to follow Carrie's example and just tell her to quit it. Public belittlement gave me the satisfaction of receiving the comeuppance I deserved.

Susan had nicknamed my apartment The Cave, yet our games therein had grown not primitive but increasingly sophisticated as we progressed from beginner spanking to intermediate applications of discipline. I barely broke a sweat and often stayed clothed throughout the session, requiring only odd bits of laundry, a few kitchen items, lubricant, and a mildly sinister imagination to keep the action moving. Susan did the work, the sweating, the whimpery emoting. Let her boss me around in front of her colleagues, call me a Richie Rich. Such indignities balanced the scale in my mind and kept my conscience clean.

It was Carrie who first tipped the balance with feelings I didn't anticipate. By no means with love, but with regard more than friendly that I couldn't square with her antagonistic sexual tack. It was one of our afternoons. Carrie had just arrived. I was in the shower when she yelled through the bathroom door that two people were here to see me. I shut off the water. "It's your neighbor and somebody else," she said.

"Is me, Philly."

"Could she come back later?" I said to Carrie.

"They say they need to speak with you."

"I have no clothes in here!" Just a bathrobe, beltless, and an expectant erection now holding in its quarter phase. I clamped the robe shut and stepped out of the bathroom. There was Mrs. Bakes in her widow's black, a fortyish woman beside her, dressed neatly and cheaply as if for a nanny's job interview.

"Forgive us," the younger woman said. "Your wife said it was okay."

"I'm not his wife," Carrie snapped.

"Something wrong, dear?" I asked her.

"You never said you were throwing people out." Evidently they'd been chatting.

"It hadn't seemed relevant to our usual dialogues."

"Cut the shit, Philip! This woman has a life."

"But no lease."

"She's lived here twenty years, she says!"

"Was my hosband's property," Mrs. Bakes jumped in. "Now is my sons'."

"And tomorrow it will be mine. I can't change that now."

"Mr. Big Shot," Carrie said. She was wearing a summer-weight jumper with nothing, I knew, underneath. Her underpants were on my bed. To the headboard were knotted my bathrobe belt and my prep school varsity letter tie. Blood fled from my face and dick.

"I don't need this from you, Carrie. Please."

"You need a kick in the butt."

"Later, I promise."

The other woman spoke: "We haven't come to beg, Mr. Halsey."

"You are?"

"My name is Melina Bakes. I'm married to Mrs. Bakes's son."

"You're Frank's wife?"

"Yes."

"The plot thickens." I regretted my flippancy at once. I was predisposed to like this woman. She was why Frank was selling the building, the Helen of Troy in the Bakes brothers' feud; as perpetrator of a family scandal, she was doubtless scorned by many, a predicament I understood. I remembered that her mother-in-law had called her a tramp. I guessed from their stances in front of me, stiff and apart, that the women were joined here uneasily, despair or guilt or dire need forcing today's alliance. My dick, to keep you posted, subsided with the onset of such sympathetic thoughts.

Melina Bakes received my dig impassively. "My mother-in-law realizes you would expect bigger rent."

"You deserve, Philly," the old woman blurted. "Is fair to make money. I can say this."

Melina continued patiently, "We understand rents must go up—"

"I pay you more, Philly! I pay six hundred, okay?"

"That's three times what she's paying now," Melina said.

"I appreciate your situation, but the numbers don't work for me. I'd be losing money on the property."

"You've only got tons," Carrie said.

"May I speak for myself, please."

"Fuck you, Philip. You're a greedy little snot."

I was appalled and embarrassed. Melina only smiled at my discomfiture—then damn if I didn't do likewise. "Look," I said, a certain warm thickness filling my throat like the first effects of an oral hallucinogen. "Mrs. Bakes has been paying two hundred a month? I'll front her six months' rent if she'll vacate in peace."

"She will not find an apartment for two hundred dollars, or even six hundred. This is the problem."

"How much, then?"

The two women conferred in whirlwind Greek before Melina suggested, "Eight hundred a month. And six months, you will offer?" As I was doing my multiplication, Carrie pounced again:

"If you can find a place around here that rents for eight hundred a month, lemme know. I'd say a thousand at least."

"Honeybunch, you're spending my money."

"I'll owe you," she winked. I had to laugh:

"All right. A thousand, times six—"

"Make it a year, Philip."

"Twelve grand!"

"Even that's not enough. Give her two."

"Two years' rent? She's not young, Carrie."

"A year-and-a-half, then."

"Eighteen months? At a thousand per?"

Carrie spun toward Mrs. Bakes and Melina. "You heard him. Philip is offering eighteen thousand dollars in severance. Are we happy?"

The three women embraced.

I scrawled a check from my stock account. When the others had left, Carrie sat beside me on the bed and put her arm around me. "Feel noble?"

"I can't even write it off."

"So your bankbook takes a small hit. Big deal."

"It's a risky time for me."

"You did a good deed today, kid. When the angels tabulate your life on a golden notebook with a crystal pencil, you may yet squeak into heaven." She smiled, saying this; nine months ago she might have been serious. My gift to her in our relationship was the little bit of incredulity that is the holiest spirit I know. Her gift to me was the doubt of my own doubts.

Carrie stroked my hair. "You were so cute when you came out of the bathroom, all angry with your bathrobe and your hard-on."

"You saw?"

"I always see. And I wanted it."

"Really?"

She was kissing me—my ear and then my mouth. Then we were on our sides face to face and I kissed her with the sloppiness of a starving man slurping fruit, a seduction impropriety that Carrie seemed not to mind. When I nudged two fingers against her vagina they slipped inside so easily I thought for a moment I'd done something wrong. "Philly," she said. "Put it in me, okay? Put it in me and come. For you."

Later we resumed our old tricks. She got on top, her hips already moving, and with a beautiful leer instructed, "Do the boy." Sometimes I think God gave us fantasy to keep our minds from wandering—during sex, I mean, for it's a curious journey thoughts can take in the middle of intercourse. This time mine didn't go far, however; just to an hour earlier when Melina Bakes was leaving. I'd asked her why she was helping her mother-in-law, since it probably wouldn't dispel Mrs. Bakes's anger toward her for rupturing the family. Melina had replied with the constraint that comes when your happiness has hurt others:

"It was something I could do."

That's the reason I surrendered $18,000 for no good reason. It was why, too, I could lie here letting Carrie possess me, saying mommy a lot and loving it; and why, on other days, I could theatrically degrade a nameless cunt named Susan and enjoy that just as much. I don't know what it means. It was something I could do.

The next day we closed on the building, "we" being Frank and Nick Bakes, the original sellers, myself the final buyer, a couple of lawyers, brokers, Lyle the office secretary, and, as buyer and seller and general ringmaster, Neil Gray of Gray Realtors.

Neil was one of those self-made men whose false modesty appears as stylized buffoonery, as if his success were a cosmic mistake instead of something he'd killed for. But give me someone falsely modest over someone comfortably proud, so I liked him. My self-esteem was cracking. I was starting to like everyone.

Neil was both buyer and seller that day because he was buying the building from Bakes Partners and then selling it to me. The closing took place at Gray Realtors. I arrived with coffee for Susan and Alison. "What are you doing here?" Alison hissed. "You're supposed to come at eleven!"

"I'm early, so what." I didn't see Susan anywhere.

"This is bad. This is so bad." Alison was a redhead. When I imagined her sexually it was all freckles and pallor and insane moans; you should hear me on black girls. I gave her her coffee and asked where was Susan.

"With Neil, in his office. They're calling the police."

"I missed something."

"There," she whispered, pointing to the open door of the office conference room. Frank Bakes, the controlling member of Bakes Partners who was forcing today's sale, was seated alone at the long table. "Neil saw he's got a gun!"

"Alison . . ."

"Okay, a bulge," she said. "Under his jacket. Look at him!"

Frank was wearing a dark suit, dark shirt, dark necktie— conceivably the uniform of a man on a mission, especially with the wraparound sunglasses. "Neil had it timed like clockwork," Alison said. "Nick was supposed to arrive first, sign the papers and leave. Then Frank, you know? So they wouldn't meet, because it's total war between them. But Nick never showed and Frank's here early—to like ambush him, we think. With the gun!"

"You takin' orders, guy?" was asked me by a fellow just out of the lavatory. He indicated the two styrofoam cups in my hands. "Coffee black for me," he said, zipping up. "And a honeybun."

Alison said to me with a frozen smile, "This is the Bakeses' attorney, Bill Kelly." As she made introductions he surveyed her from head to toe; I saw his filthy redhead fantasies bubble up like sludge. Alison described me as "Buyer number two."

"I heard Neil was pulling a quickie," Kelly laughed.

"He's taking a loss," I explained.

"He tell you that?"

"Cool it, Bill," she said. "You guys weren't even supposed to meet."

To counter his insinuation with one of my own, I said to Kelly uppishly, "Alison had a question about your client. She was concerned that he brought a handgun with him this morning. Could you check?"

"Hey, Frankie!" he bellowed across the office. "You carryin' heat?" Brokers turned at their desks. Frank Bakes gazed at us. "A weapon, guy? You carryin'?"

Frank's glasses reflected the overhead lights. "I wish," he said softly. Alison wasn't convinced:

"What about his bulge? Ask him."

Bill Kelly looked at her, then back at Frank. "Girl says you gotta bulge, Frankie. Talk to her." He headed for the conference room, me and Alison following.

Frank, in answer, took a pint bottle from his coat pocket, uncapped it and raised a toast. His smile crumpled suddenly and tears spilled from under his sunglasses. His lawyer went to him and massaged one shoulder, Alison the other, as Frank broke down and sobbed. I observed from the doorway, sipping Susan's decaf. Awkward in these situations, I've learned from experience to find something to do, lest I break out laughing.

Neil Gray's office door kicked open and out he came, short

57

and bald in a custom suit. Through an iron grin he whispered to me, "The cops are coming. Act normal." When I told him the cops wouldn't be needed, he whirled on Susan behind him. "Call and cancel. Cops and lawyers together I can*not* handle."

"I phoned them for you. You phone them back."

"Humor me, huh? Pretend I'm the boss."

"The idiot, you mean."

"Idiot!"

"That's right. Idiot and . . . pifflehead!" Susan was giggling like a midwestern cheerleader, a side of her only Neil elicited.

He grabbed his chest. "Not pifflehead! Not that! And in front of the clients," he added, meaning me.

"I'm hurt," I said, playing along. "Surely we're past such formality."

He slapped me on the back. "Absolutely! Me and Philip," he waved a fist to the room like a cornered politician: "Like brothers!" I draped my arm around him. Who is this guy, I thought. We'd met a couple times before, and he was unlike any executive I'd ever known, loony and childlike, with an edge. I attributed my sense of Neil's strangeness to my sheltered Boston upbringing; to his being Jewish, in other words, for in my youth I'd known Jews exactly never (not counting my father, which was his wish). It took college to teach me what a bagel was, and my Jewish first year roommate was WASPier than I in his quest for the perfect shiksa, his heritage, like mine, mentioned only in jokes and in adamant holy-day skepticism. Between freshman and sophomore year, however, he took a craving for history and joined a kibbutz in Israel. He sent me a photo of himself in a vegetable patch. He wrote that Israeli girls were beautiful and that he was quitting the kibbutz for the army because the army had more girls than the kibbutz. Lastly he said I was wasting my life, this from a kid off a commune. The following year Israel invaded Lebanon. I looked for him on the TV news among soldiers manning checkpoints or shepherding refugees. I never saw him; the odds against it were huge, and given the years and changes between us, I'm sure I wouldn't have recognized him.

Through the front window of the realty office, I saw a

black-and-white squad car pull up. Two cops strolled in. Neil shouted, "Hide the dope!"

They smiled. One said, "We got a call—"

"Where's your bulletproof vests, men? What I donated for those things, I expect you guys to wear 'em. It's like my wife—I buy her clothes, she don't wear 'em! Says they make her look like a hooker. I say, Yeah, so?"

"False alarm, sir?"

Neil was contrite. "I hallucinated, that's all I can figure. I'm old. Today I see guns, tomorrow the reaper." He reached for his wallet. "A double-sawbuck for your trouble?"

"Another time," the cop said. He and his partner left, swaggering as well they should, though I prefer it going away.

My lawyer arrived. His name was Jeffrey Masters. Susan had recommended him, and at our first meeting he'd been disarmingly candid about his fee and his brilliance. Right behind Jeffrey came Nick Bakes. Nick wore pizza-chef whites and brandished his car keys before him as an exorcist might a crucifix. His brother Frank had removed his sunglasses, revealing eyes that burned as they tracked his wife's chosen. Bill Kelly and Alison stood by like hired protection. I wondered what I was doing here.

Neil clapped his hands. "My timing's kaput but let's do it. Let's make some money."

"Neil," I said. "About that—you *are* taking a loss on our deal?"

"Why would I?"

"Susan implied—"

"The loss she's talking about is what I could have got for the property, had I held out for my price. Relative to what you're paying, yes. I'm taking a significant loss."

I nodded, confused. "It was a question I had."

"I want you to be comfortable."

It's fair, I thought as he walked away. He's a businessman and—it crossed my mind—he's a Jew. A real estate Jew. He isn't Santa Claus. Susan approached me. "Excited?"

"Terrified."

"That's understandable. Frank and Nick haven't seen each

other since the breakup. You can feel the anger." She shivered. "It's, I don't know—"

"A turn-on?"

She gave me a stony look. Jeffrey Masters came up behind her, pulling papers from his briefcase. "While we're doing the deed with the Bakeses, Philip, you wanna read this and sign it? It's a release, says you agree to my representing both parties in your closing, Neil and you."

"A release?"

"I told you I work for Neil, right?"

"I told him," Susan said.

"It's not often done, and it can look odd, but in a casual deal like today, no problem."

"Casual," I echoed.

"Exactly. I'm also representing the bank, of course. Your loan check came this morning. You brought the balance, I trust, and a checkbook for incidentals."

"I do. I did."

"You okay, buddy?"

"It's his first closing," Susan explained.

Jeffrey got wistful. "I remember my first. It was sweet. Anyway," he continued, "regarding evictions—the letters are drafted. I'll drive one over to Nick's Pizza after we close. My secretary will hand deliver the other one to the old lady this afternoon. My guess is they'll ignore us. Next we hit 'em with a cease-and-desist. It's a process. Eight weeks tops and they're out."

"Can't you give Nick his notice right now?"

"You're not the owner yet."

"Gotcha."

"Incidentally, Philip—your suggestions as to the wording on those eviction letters? Primo. Classy yet blunt. I'm keeping them as guidelines for the future."

"It's a knack. I was born to persecute."

"Don't be weird," Susan said.

"I *feel* weird." In fact I felt afraid. I couldn't bring myself to tell them I'd royally paid off Mrs. Bakes to vacate her apartment. They'd mark me a fool, and rightly.

Jeffrey said to me tenderly, "This thing today is cake. One hour and you'll be a real estate entrepreneur. Revel in it! This is the 1980s!" When I smiled he gave me the high sign: "*Sweet.*"

"What's wrong with you?" Susan asked when he'd left. "You act like you're on death row."

"I'm not used to real estate. I feel vulnerable."

"Fake it."

"That's not what I need from you." I needed her to break code and touch me, give a reassuring stroke to my wrist or jacket sleeve. No one was watching, surely it would be all right. But the only plea I could verbalize covered our usual topic. "Tell me the building's a bargain and it'll make me money." Tonelessly, she recited it back to me:

"The building's a bargain and it will make you money."

"You're dear to say that, Susan."

I took a seat outside the conference room. Jeffrey's release reminded me of releases I'd signed three years earlier, of my father and Stalls Associates. Absolving them in the event of my financial failure was a smart move in retrospect. As a fortunate son in fortunate times, I was hard-pressed for woe. Young people traditionally encounter trauma that amputates the fledgling past and leaves a phantom pang, a permanent intimation of one's lost innocence; maturity results. But unblessed with a war to fight or bereavement to endure, I'd created my trauma in accordance with what was available. I was certain that my attorney had conspired with Neil and Susan to sell me a bogus building. So be it. If my suspicion proved wrong, I'd settle for success. If correct, I was prepared for the Plan B of growing wiser for the experience.

Noise came from the conference room. I heard Frank Bakes curse his brother, heard Neil shout, "Let's be men!" More oaths followed, then the voices of lawyers trying to referee. Lyle the office secretary was manning the phones across from me. "Tragic," he said, catching my eye.

I nodded. Lyle was gay. To avoid any misconception I was generally rude to him. He seemed to pity me for it, but better that than the other, I figured.

"I've seen the building you're buying. You won't be sorry."
I perked up. "You think?"
"In this area? Can't miss."
"Evicting people is no fun."
"I don't imagine it is."
"Matter of fact, I paid one to leave."
"Bought out the lease?"
"She didn't have a lease. I was buying peace of mind, basically."
"Your secret's safe with me."
It had grown quiet in the conference room. The door pushed open and Alison came out as if tiptoeing from a nursery. She shut the door and rolled her eyes. "You won't believe what's happening in there. Frank—he's drunk, right?—one second he yells, the next second he bawls. He got on his knees and begged Nick to send his wife back. In front of everyone, *begged.* I couldn't watch." She went to her desk for Kleenex.
"What'd you expect?" Lyle said. "He's heartbroken."
"I have sympathy for the guy, but show a little backbone."
"Backbone is for liars. Frank is in agony."
"How's Nick holding up?" I asked her.
"Says not a word. Totally noble."
"Sure," Lyle said. "He's the winner. He has what he wants."
"Sometimes it's harder to be the bad guy than the victim," I said.
Lyle laughed. "You have to say that."
"What the hell does that mean?"
"It means you've never been hurt."
"Now boys," Alison said, turning toward the conference room.
"You're going back in?"
"They need Kleenex. And I wouldn't miss it."
It was me and Lyle alone again. He typed and I reread my lawyer's release. Now and then I glanced up at him and dealt him a punishing glare. "Relax, Philip. I'm not the enemy."
This threw me. "Who is?"
The door flew open and Nick Bakes emerged, pursued by a howl: "How long you fock her! How long I'm a jackass!" Nick took a chair beside mine. His face was sweaty.

"He's not doing so good, my brother."

Lyle typed reprovingly.

I asked Nick, "They about done in there?"

"I sign the paper. I get my check in a minute." In my acquaintance as the man behind the pizza counter, Nick had been jovial most of the time and gushing when I paid my rent. Lately, however, his clash of remorse and illicit joy had been manifested in a mishmash of inappropriate humors and long, unfocused stares, one of which was aimed my way right now. I became uncomfortable:

"I met your—your what?"

"My Melina? She tell me. You give her much money yesterday. For my mother."

"It was something I could do. I guess your mother's looking for a new apartment to rent?"

"She decide to live with me and Melina. We make an addition, a room for herself." With my $18,000? Swindler!

"I thought your mom and Melina didn't like each other."

"Is better now."

"I'll bet." Annoyance made me pushy: "I thought your mother was taking Frank's side through all this."

"She must watch for herself, too. Where she gonna live?"

"She can live with Frank."

"No one can live with Frank. And she's afraid a little. His problem."

"Ohhh. He's a boozer."

"You know nothing about it! He's all the time angry, Frank. Like our father."

"Today oughta cheer him up." His eyes narrowed at my sarcasm:

"You tease with me? Because if you tease with me, you make a mistake. Me and Frank and Melina is not for your fun."

"I'm not teasing you. Come on, we've always been friends."

"I sell you pizza. Big shit."

"Our relationship has been more than that to me. It's been a welcome part of my day, my life." I couldn't help sounding condescending—the preposterousness of my words demanded it. The sad part was, I meant to be genuine. I did consider Nick and me friends, had relished the chat about sports and weather that had bonded us as men while I awaited my mushroom-bacon. His dismissal stung me like a lover's rejection. In a reflex of wanting to sting him back, I brought up the future of his pizza business. "Soon there will be medical offices upstairs," I told him. "I've been advised that pizza is no go as a retail tenant. Purely image, I'm talking."

"You kick me out?"

"I like you, Nick. I like your pizza. But you haven't got a lease." Now he pulls the knife, I thought.

"I figure this," he said mildly.

"Can you relocate?"

"This location is beautiful for me. To move? No."

"The building's in a valuable spot, isn't it?"

He studied me. "Not bad. You wanna sell?"

"I think not."

"The place needs work."

"It'll pay off." I was happy again, feeling fine on two unsolicited shots of approval—from a fag and a Greek backslider, true, but I was grateful for anything. Nick slapped his knee as if relieved.

"Okay, Philly. You kick me out. I tell my people when?"

"You're going to fire your workers?"

"Not your fault. Frank say it to me he will do this."

"Doesn't seem fair, does it?"

"For my workers, no. For me?" He sighed. "Is fair."

"Because of your affair with Melina?"

His look of anger at my mentioning this passed—Frank had spilled the news all over town. And Nick's silence told me it was because of Melina: her love, its price, his need to pay it. I was touched. Nick's penitence was the real thing, its prideful armor rendering it still more affecting. Clearly he had regrets about betraying his brother, and clearly he'd do it again in the same situation. No redemption, no hope of forgiveness, none of that salvation guff—just the bleak satisfaction of accepting the penalty commensurate with the prize. At which thought I got an idea. Nick needn't be penalized at all. I could reward him, spare him. With the added relief, too, of easing my own apprehensions about some of the choices I'd taken in life, and some of the consequences I'd so far avoided. Let me remain the holy sinner. Let Nick be another of God's undeserving lucky ones.

"Tell me," I asked him. "Is there a business you know besides pizza? Something snazzy. Say, a boutique?"

No answer.

"A boutique. You know: ladies' underwear, soap."

He shook his head.

"Does Melina?"

"Underwear? Not so much."

"Does she work?"

"In a flower shop. Downtown."

"Perfect! Turn the pizza place into a flower shop, you and her. There's nothing like it around here, and with all the yuppies and condos sprouting, you'll make a fortune."

He considered. "Is possible. And how much rent to pay?"

"Well, it's got to kick up some. Economics."

"We can share gross."

"I'm hesitant. Partnerships stink, as you know. But forget the details. You must sell your fixtures and order new. You have cash to capitalize, I assume—at least eighteen grand, right? So it's done, you're a florist." I was pleased. I'd saved him, taken his sin on myself just like Jesus. "You're Nick's Flowers now."

He shook his head. "Melina's Little Bud Shop."

"Nice," I said. At his desk Lyle started to clap.

"Bravo, gentlemen. You have touched my heart."

"You shouldn't eavesdrop, Lyle."

"How could I not? And let me say, it was beautiful."

I thanked him, thanked Nick, then leaned back in my chair, exhausted. Anticlimax brought doubt and an old foreboding, and like Lyle said, it was beautiful.

Exiting the conference room, everyone looked beat and relieved, save Frank who seemcd merely beat and Susan who seemed Susan, brisk as an eyewitness newsperson and looking every inch the imperial Jewess. It's not a nice term, "Jewess," conferring anthropologic distinction as Custer conferred it on Indians. But what was she to me if not a threatening exotic? With no clue to her center I'd stuck her, as with arrows, with rancorous labels, "Jewess" joining "bitch" and "cunt" and "real estate broker" as blind attempts to pinpoint her. "Mother of my child" came later, and proved my biggest miss.

She was watching me watch her. "What's funny?"

"Nothing." Ambivalence had put a grin on my face. "Did I tell you, you look good today."

"I always look good." Typical, but this time said with her hand on my shoulder, high warmth for Susan. I laid my hand over hers, my pulse accelerating at this forbidden public display. "Rough scene in there?"

"Pretty rough. It was scary, all that emotion."

"All that pathology."

She smiled. "It made me appreciate my husband. He's becoming more modulated these days, more sane. Like you."

"I prefer to think of myself as incredibly fucked up."

"Him too, believe me—fucked up on religion, on the rigors of his faith. He has Judaism where you have money."

"Of course there's no comparison."

"Defending your rival?"

"I've always conceded the high road. And I didn't know we were rivals."

"Never presume, Philip."

"What's his name again? The new one."

"It's Gershom. As you well know."

"Right. Gershom. Good ol' Gersh."

"Don't be an ass." She hesitated. "I saw him last night. He came by my apartment."

"Okay."

"We talked—"

"It happens, go on."

"—about things."

"Susan!" Her drama maddened me. "Gershom wants you back and you said yes. Go in peace, baby. I'll survive."

"I said no."

"Oh. Did he freak?"

"He was very calm about it. Unusually so."

"Reverse psychology."

"Not his style. He asked me to come back and I said no. I had to."

"Had to?" I felt flattered. "Why?"

She gave me a look I can only call magical, transforming her before my eyes from empress to maiden to puddle. "I'll explain when we're alone," she said.

I was sitting and she was standing in front of me, so when I raised my palm to the front of her skirt it was rather a salute. Between her legs the skirt material gave. I pressed into the Y of her groin and she pressed back and there occurred, through layers of natural fibers, contact. Her pubic bone throbbed like an engine. I looked up, she down, the antithesis of our sexual postures—and in the meeting of our eyes unspoken secrets were shared. Two different secrets, however. To me the message seemed clear: She wanted me more than she wanted her marriage, hence she'd "had to" snub Gershom. But Susan, perhaps rendered mute by her gynecologist's confirmation, was on another wavelength entirely. My touch must have surprised her with its tender presumption, must have led her to believe I'd sensed the truth and was lovingly endorsing it. I was thinking pussy, she was thinking womb. It was a simple mistake.

As I worked the heel of my hand, she murmured dreamily, "I hated you this morning. That's why I was a bitch before."

"And I hated you. I'd convinced myself the building was a rip-off and you knew it."

"Who cares about that now?"

"I'm wrong, I trust."

"Jesus, you never stop."

"It's on my mind, okay? It's a big day for me."

She withdrew her crotch from reach. "A big day for you?"

"I'm glad we agree."

"And what happens next?"

"After this? We meet at my place and fuck like pigs in a gutter. Then food."

She shook her head violently, as if denying bad news. "My God, I don't even know you."

"That's why our relationship works! Ambivalence is hot. You need danger, a door to unlock to keep it exciting."

"What are you talking about?"

"You have to ask? I'm talking about us, me and you and the ol' one-two." My poetry didn't impress her:

"Eat shit, Philip."

"Recess is over, kids," said Neil Gray, approaching. "Let's make Philip—"

"Disappear," Susan suggested.

"—a landlord, I was gonna say. Whatsa matter?"

"Philip and I were just wallowing in the grotesque." The melting in Susan's face of moments before had reversed itself, as when snow softens and then refreezes and takes a glittery crust. I was wishing she'd yell or laugh at me, poke out her tongue like a winter seedling, a harbinger of warmth to come. She glanced at Neil and he nodded, not comprehending but agreeing. It was two against one. To even the odds I called over my new friend and business associate, Nick Bakes.

"Nick. Tell them I'm not a schmuck." His brother shadowed him, steadying himself against the furniture.

"What you mean?" Nick said.

"Tell them my plan for your store. Our plan."

"For rent?"

"For flowers, man! Don't go foreign on me." This angered him into clamming up.

Susan said, "Real sweet, Philip."

Lyle helped me out. "He cut Nick a deal. He's—hey!"

Frank Bakes lunged past Lyle's desk toward us. He grabbed me before I knew it. His arms around me, his stubble scraping my face, I realized he intended affection. He addressed his brother in English that we all might share the moment. "To see you on the street, Nikos—this is my pride! I sell everything I work for to bring you trouble and trouble for Melina." He gave me a squeeze. He breath smelled of liquor though not of rot, which is why I'm alive today. "Here is my pride! Philly will put you and your pizza shit on the street. He can break your heart like you break mine."

Nick said nothing. I knew he wanted out of here, let stand

his brother's illusion. Words blew out of me in an ill-conceived attempt to restore my standing with Susan:

"Sorry to disappoint you, Frank—but I'm letting Nick stay. He and I are friends, and out of friendship I've offered him a new lease. Him and Melina." Aiming at the others, I said, "The dollar comes second with me."

I heard their murmurs, but what fascinated me was Frank; it was like holding someone underwater and watching his face turn color. I explained the flower shop thing and he went red and blue. But just as I thought he was about to pass out, he exhaled and burst out laughing. I laughed with him, afraid to do otherwise, as he raucously pounded my back.

"Philly! From you the hand of God hits me, eh? Hits me and raises my brother and my whore-for-a-wife. Frank is for shit and they are for the angels. I can laugh to see this."

I was speechless. Neil spoke up quickly, "So we're settled. Everyone's happy." To end the episode, punctuate it with a moral, he added, "How hapless a lover's revenge." This drew more glee from Frank, his humor snowballing, gathering ice and grit.

"The Jewish tells me about revenge. Funny, eh Philly?"

I gave the others a look to say I didn't know this man.

"He's right," Frank persisted, still hugging me. "The Jewish steals from me my father's property and jokes how I am helpless."

"*Hapless*, I said." Neil's face was expressionless. "If I offended you, I'm sorry."

"Don't apologize to him!" Susan snapped.

"They didn't steal anything," I said to Frank. "They're fine people. They bought your building fair and square." This freed me from his hug but won me no friend in Neil or Susan, who hadn't appreciated my "they." Frank didn't help matters:

"They get you too, Philly. What you make, they make twice."

"I'm perfectly satisfied."

"*I'm perfectly satisfied*," he sneered. "You so fancy, like a woman."

Terrific, I thought—and without wearing an earring, even!

"Why don't you just leave," Susan told him.

"That'd be best," Neil agreed, whereupon Frank erupted:

"You fock you, Jew! I got nothing, not nothing!" His words repulsed them visibly, like grapeshot through innocent bystanders.

"You've got a check in your hand for $90,000 clean!" Neil retorted. "Tell me you got nothing? Baloney! I paid the price you agreed to." His words notwithstanding, his voice was defensive, taut with self-blame that I felt in myself as well. Frank was wounded, heartsick—in his blind desire to hurt his brother he'd sold his property at a fire-sale price. Perhaps the ugliness he spoke was forgivable, even warranted. To me Frank was a lowlife joke; to Neil he was a sap. Had we given him cause to hate us? Bigotry's dirtiest trick must be the way it makes you wonder.

Frank was set to spew again when his brother intervened. In bursts of Greek they raged at each other and we watched it like a tennis match. Then Nick said something that must have scored. Frank suddenly wilted, dropping to his knees before Neil. "I am not really hating you, mister. You will forget me please?"

"Forgive, he means to say," Nick said.

"Whatever," Neil said. "Just get him to stand and leave. This scene is too nutty."

"You will forgive?" Frank wailed, tugging Neil's jacket.

"Yes, okay! Go forth and prosper, be happy—but go!"

Frank stood. "I am not happy. I will remember today every day."

His attorney Bill Kelly consoled him. "Chin up, guy. Forget the bitch."

"You shut up like that!"

"Whoa, pardner! No offense. Call me." Kelly left with a last leer at Alison.

Frank and Nick faced a decision. They couldn't leave together, yet for one of them to leave alone, first, might cast him as the coward. Delaying a moment, they postponed the estrangement they would awaken to each morning from now on, awaken foggy, momentarily hopeful, as if after an operation in which body parts were amputated. The seconds that passed were sufficient for poignancy, the brothers' mutual reluctance evident, before Frank went to Nick, seized his shoulders, said a Greek goodbye, then hesitated. I thought sure he would kiss him, but Frank was Frank and none too subtle, so spat full in his brother's face, turned on a heel and left. Nick wiped his face with a shirtsleeve, aware he'd gotten off easy.

Neil had covered his eyes. "Tell me he's gone."

"He's gone," Susan said.

Neil pointed at Nick. "I don't like your brother."

"Of course."

"He's got a sewer for a mouth. What did you say to shut him up?" Receiving no answer, Neil pressed him angrily: "What'd you say, Save it for later? We'll string the Jew up later?"

"I say it to him he is talking like our father."

"Pop was a gem, huh?" The expression puzzled Nick, who looked to me to translate.

"Neil is saying he doesn't like your dad either."

Nick nodded. "Frank same. Our father was bad to him."

A long silence followed. Neil clapped his hands, "Gee, I'd love to compare notes on family psychology, but you understand—I have other schemes to hatch."

"Forget it, Neil," his lawyer soothed him. "These people are nothing."

"Is fine," Nick said. "I go."

I reminded him of our flower deal. "It's firm as far as I'm concerned. You're still my tenant. We'll talk tomorrow."

Nick gave a quick nod. I didn't expect more. Thanks to me, this morning had brought him an unexpected windfall for which, for a change, he'd hurt no one's feelings nor committed no sin. He was too modest to gloat.

"Do I understand, then," Jeffrey Masters said to me, "that you won't be evicting Nick's Pizza?"

"Or his mother. I paid her to vacate voluntarily."

"How much?" Susan asked.

"Eighteen. Thousand."

"Holy Christ," Jeffrey said.

Neil said to Susan, "I thought you said Philip was tight?"

"I thought he was. Cheap car, cheap clothes—"

"Big heart," I suggested. Susan turned away to hide her smile. She liked me, was the problem; I think it sickened her. I shrugged to Neil, "Pretty dumb, huh? To give it away like that?"

"What can I say? You're a better man than I am."

Jeffrey was worried. "Uh, Philip—on those eviction letters? I've put in some hours."

"Bill me."

"Will do." He grinned at Neil. "We're set, boss! He's done the dirty work, let's bust the deal and move in. Negotiating with tenants prior to purchase? Looks like breach of contract. We can walk away right now." Jeffrey giggled as fear ripped through me. "Just kidding, Philip. But what a pigeon! Be glad you're among friends."

I exhaled. "Indeed."

We started for the conference room. Susan had wandered to the front of the office. Standing before a picture window, her profile outlined in light, she looked flawless and unattainable, like a lingerie model. I wanted to eat her, kiss her cheek; I felt distance between us and was willing to bridge it any way possible. Neil called to her, "It's your sale, honey. Let's go."

"You don't need me."

I complained, "It's my first closing. My broker's supposed to comfort me."

"You're a big boy."

"You'll be here when we're done?"

She dragged her eyes from the window to me. "Where else? The mall?"

I saw Lyle go over to talk with her. They huddled comfortably, his hand on the small of her back. When she nodded at something he said, I was jealous. It was the image itself: two young people whispering in the frame of a lighted window. It compared with holding hands and spending a whole night together, things I'd never done with Susan or anyone else.

The closing went fast, money and papers exchanged like playing cards. Susan was waiting when we came out. She asked me how it went. "I'm the landed gentry now."

"Congratulations."

"I owe it to you."

"We should talk. Lyle says you deserve a second chance."

"I'm sure he's right."

"Philip!" someone called behind me. "Phone."

At this interruption a moment was missed. Had it been anything else I would have remained with Susan, heard her out. But the caller was Timmy Donley and the news, of the stock market, was bad. The Fed Funds rate had risen and the Dow was falling in reflex. A hefty position I'd taken in S & P futures was eroding as we spoke. I had to be there, at the brokerage, the market my time and tide. Susan was not sympathetic.

"I need a lousy minute! Our signals got crossed before."

"I know, and we'll talk. I promise."

"Goddamn it!"

"Hold that thought. I'll call you." And out the door I went. A mistake? Yes and no. I chose the right crisis if you discount human feelings. They say pregnancy makes a woman glow. I well remember Susan's look through the window as I got into my car. I wouldn't call it glowing.

The honeymoon lasted six days. That is, the dream union of commercial real estate and my securities investments was, by the seventh day, no longer fun. Yet that first blush of enterprise makes a memory that, in the words of decrepit sports champions, no one can take away.

I knew what I was doing and why, those first days. I helped Mrs. Bakes move out and moved myself as well. I took a room over a Chinese restaurant, bigger than my old place, with an air conditioner. In keeping with such improved circumstances, I upgraded my wardrobe from thrift shop to Armani. As for Szechuan every day, my system protested but soon came to love it.

I stayed tuned to the market, temporarily bearish, while popping over to the building several times daily. An excavating crew was flattening the back garages and the embankment behind them, for parking. The crew was African American. Hovering over the working men, I felt like a plantation dandy. Their sweat and their Kools, the picks and shovels and machinery roar, combined to quite unsettle me in my Vuarnets and tennis shorts. They addressed me as Mr. Halsey with no apparent malice and for this. I was thankful yet oddly let down, knowing money confers respect before you're able to earn it. One day I ascended a large dirt pile to survey my quarter-acre and several workmen laughed, asking if I wanted my picture taken. I enjoyed the ribbing, the fraternity. That afternoon I brought them a case of malt liquor and refused their money, drinking myself into much fellow-feeling and calling them brother out loud. When the party broke up, the foreman took me aside and respectfully asked me to keep my distance in the future. My presence was bugging his men, he said.

The next day, the sixth day, I arrived after the work crew had left. I found that the men had uncovered an abandoned well within the embankment, a stone-lined cylinder maybe ten feet deep and buried at the top under two feet of earth. The front-loader had cleaved the embankment vertically, revealing the well in cross-section like an ant-farm tunnel. It was a forlorn-looking structure, like those stone walls you see in New England, back-breaking projects evidently worthwhile to colonial homesteaders when they were living, yet which today, overgrown and collapsed, disappear in impassable forests where no wall would serve any use. The discovery of the well seemed a good excuse to phone Susan. We hadn't talked since the closing. I thought a newsy pretense would break any ice that had formed. But she was sweet as could be, as impressed with the well as if I'd struck oil, and said she wanted to come see it. I apologized for not calling sooner. "You've been busy," she said. "Just be there tomorrow."

That next day, Saturday, the workmen were off. On the cleared ground behind my building the front-loader and bulldozer sat silent and hulking with their shovels at rest like warriors laying down arms. I heard a motor in the alley, then a radio blaring the Red Sox game. A pickup truck appeared. A gaggle of undergrads was piled in back, outfitted for an archeological dig in cutoffs and boots and a milk-fed ruddiness I associate with environmentalists. The driver was different—in his beard and yarmulke, he was decidedly urban compared to his Greenpeacenik passengers. I should have sensed a trick immediately, but as I'm slow to get punch lines, I was slow to get wise as to who he was and what sort of foul joke had been played, until the young man spoke in his father's voice:

"You must be Philip. I'm Gershom Graulig."

I was cool. She couldn't have told him—

"So you're Susan's lover. Interesting."

"It can be." My best shot. After that I was mush.

"I haven't come to fight. I've come to excavate your well, if that's all right."

"Is it valuable?"

"To oddballs like me and my students. I doubt you could convert it to stock certificates."

"That a joke?"

He laughed uncomfortably; how dispiriting it must have been to find his wife was fucking a moron. "A bad joke. Anyway—"

"Susan told you what I do? In business."

"She said you play the market. Sounds great."

I thought sure Gershom would attack me any second. He didn't appear armed, though his students unloading their digging tools had brought blunt objects to spare. "What do you teach?" I asked suspiciously.

"This is a sociology seminar. 'Toward a Suburban Aesthetic: Lifestyle Trends Since 1950.'"

"This isn't the suburbs."

"It was once."

"Well, I must tell you, Gershom. I'm reluctant to disrupt my workers."

"They're not here."

"Yes, but a bunch of amateurs messing about their turf might upset them, I think."

"We'd be doing them a favor. We dig out the well and the embankment above it and that's less they have to do Monday. We've examined some of the biggest construction sites in the city and trust me, no one's complained."

"Examined for what?"

"For history. For societal structure as evidenced through artifacts, building foundations, garbage dumps. We're creating a chronological grid of neighborhood evolution, from production economies to service economies to regions of pure habitation. I'm locating precursors to President Reagan's Enterprise Zones, so-called. You've heard of them?"

"I think only Reagan has."

"Too right. But even if never implemented, they permit conservatives a rhetoric of social concern which must be revealed for the hogwash it is." He was heating up, but let him, I thought; better public affairs than private. "Promoting industrial growth in dying communities can only help if decent, low-cost housing is available. Otherwise labor festers in tenements outside the factory walls while management flees for the suburbs. The precedents exist throughout our history. Lack of housing is what destroys a community. Provide it and the rest will come: growth, security, and neighborhood pride. But it takes active government investment, and Reagan's blind to that. Willfully, criminally blind."

"I like the man."

"What's not to like? But he's careless as a child. Until his regime is ousted, people are going to suffer."

"They'll suffer anyway."

"Will you?"

"Not if I can help it." His onlooking students laughed— a coed group of eight, probably half of them law school-bound, no matter their ecopretensions. My debate with their instructor had devolved to me versus him, a contest that I, not caring if I won, couldn't lose. My stake here was purely stylistic. Though Gershom had me beat on virtue, I got the laughs and the girl, his girl. Susan was my ace in the hole, a card he couldn't top. It was as if, provoked, I could have pulled out my dick and shamed him with its size and power, ending all argument. In truth I never would have tried this. These short guys can surprise you.

Generous in victory, I gave Gershom permission to examine the well. As we walked over to it, he spied me studying his hair. "I know. It's thinning."

"I was checking out the skullcap. Is that a bobby pin?"

"It is."

"What's it for, exactly."

"It affixes the yarmulke to my head."

"I mean the cap."

"So God can pick us out in a crowd."

"Us being Jews?"

He stopped and looked at me. "You don't get jokes, do you?"

"I have wit but no sense of humor."

"Susan says *I* have no sense of humor."

"That can't be the difference, then."

He divided his people into two groups, one to inspect above the embankment for foundations or dump sites, the other to sift excavated soil for artifacts. But the second chore couldn't be done. "You sold your topsoil?" he asked me.

"My what?"

"Your topsoil. There must have been a lot of it."

Glancing around, I saw that the dirt pile I'd climbed two days earlier was gone, removed. "It was in the way," I shrugged. "There was tons of it."

"I hope you got a good price."

"You don't get much for dirt, Gershom."

"Are you kidding? Around here, good topsoil is gold. Twenty bucks a yard, at least. How many yards did you have?"

"Who cares? It was a pile of dirt."

"Jill!" Gershom called to a girl on the upper embankment. "How much soil you think they scraped? Her dad's a landscaper," he told me. His eyes had taken an evil shine. Jill, above us, looked like a landscaper's daughter as she surveyed the area. At length she concluded, "Four hundred."

"Dollars?" I laughed. "Hardly worth worrying about."

"Four hundred cubic yards. Possibly more."

Gershom did the math. "Eight thousand dollars. Gosh." I closed my eyes as the horror passed through me. I heard Gershom explain, "His excavators took all his topsoil."

"Didn't he know?"

"He didn't know."

"So I didn't know! Now I know, and I'll take care of it. The workmen are buddies of mine."

Gershom looked grave and helpful. "It'll be fine, I'm sure."

"Thanks, Gersh."

He dispatched the second group of students to the properties behind my own, rundown brownstones of uncertain vintage. He told them to note architectural styles and to rough out a demographic profile. They skipped to their work happy-go-luckily, like scientists on a government grant. Then Gershom said to me, "Susan calls me Gersh sometimes. Do you mean it as an insult, too?"

"I have no reason to insult you."

"Nor I you." That did it for me:

"Can we fight now? This gentleman stuff is scary."

"I'm sorry you feel that way."

"You should hate my guts."

"Nonsense. Regarding Susan and me, you're a minor player, a plot device. The stage was set for upheaval long before you appeared. You could have been anyone."

"Then regarding Susan and me, *you're* a minor player. How does it feel?"

"It feels like the truth."

"You're impossible."

"What, you want me to hate you?"

"It's something I understand."

"My capacity for hatred is all used up." He fixed one eye on me. "Not on Susan. It's myself I've hated."

"Because you weren't better for her?"

"Because my best wasn't good enough."

"Rule number one: Never give your best."

"Keep your wisdom. I'll survive without it."

"The faith helps, I imagine."

"The faith?"

"The skullcap. The new name."

"Susan told you I changed my name? That's worse than sleeping with you."

"What was it before? Something Irish."

"It was Gerald."

"Gerald to Gershom? That really blows off the past."

"In fact it honors it."

"Minus your father."

His eyes widened. "Do I have any secrets?"

"Tell you what, I'll share. My real name is Holscheimer. I changed it three years ago."

"Bull."

"I swear to God."

"Why?"

"To get girls. Halsey's cooler."

"You are a jerk."

"It worked."

"You're determined to provoke me. I don't know why."

"To save your marriage, possibly?" I posed my hint as a question. The truth I wanted him to infer was that things could work out if he wanted. Merely say the word, perhaps launch a mild physical assault—he could have his woman back. Clearly Susan and I were a limited proposition, so from my end the scenario had its appeal. Trifling with love and yet destroying no one would seem the perfect crime.

"But if I wanted to fight for Susan, I would. I don't."

"I thought you loved her."

"I needed her. That's different."

"And now?"

"I have my faith, as you say—and my work."

"Methadone."

"Worthy substitutes. Time well spent." He smiled. "I'm not obsessed with her, if that's what you think."

"Your wife told me different."

"Did she?" He stopped smiling. "I could hit her, I swear."

"Now you're talking."

"Okay, so I went a little nuts. I followed her, I tapped her phone—"

"You tapped her phone!"

"I have a friend in electrical engineering. Susan never knew."

"Find any dirt?"

"Zip. She didn't need to phone him, anyway. They see each other every day."

"You have a suspect? Besides me?"

"You came later. By then I was numb."

"Someone at work, eh? Lyle forget, so—" It hit me. "Your father?"

"I have no proof."

"Susan and your father!"

Gershom shrugged and turned away—in shame, no doubt.

"Listen. I've met Neil. Slippery, maybe. But he's not evil."

"What evil? He's silly. He's a silly, immature man."

"But seduce his son's wife!"

"It's worse than that. Neil is in love with her. From afar, understand? He's noble about it!" Gershom paused to calm himself. "Susan knew my insecurities regarding him. She played on them, me against him. Everything he did was just *so* amusing, *so* clever. Maybe you've seen—with him she's animated, girlish. With him she's happy, and he laps it up."

"The man is a newlywed!"

"Dominique? Poor woman, she's the victim here."

"I was told you didn't like her."

"She's terrific! I was hoping Neil would be content with her. But he's made her a surrogate. That's why he's always buying her things—in apology. He mocks love constantly, but inside he's a sentimental maniac. For Susan."

"Susan can't know, that's all."

"She knows. It's a joke to her, it's preposterous—so she's careless. She leads him on."

"If she knew his feelings, she'd laugh in his face."

"You sure?"

"No."

"See."

My head spun. "What about me? I have feelings. I matter here. She and I are going steady!"

"You're a blip. You're nothing. So was I till I walked away. Now I'm free."

"Free to fixate on God and dirt."

"Get it straight, Philip. I don't fixate."

80

"The skullcap, Gershom. It speaks volumes."

"I'm a student of Judaism. If that bothers you, goodbye."

"It interests me. If you were wearing a crucifix I'd wonder about that—or a shrunken head, or love beads."

"You're nonpracticing, I take it."

"A nonpracticing Holscheimer, yes."

"Still, you know what day it is. My being here proves I'm not fanatical." His meaning eluded me. "Today is the Sabbath, dummy. Work is a no-no, strictly speaking."

"You're not working. Your students are."

In retort he grabbed a shovel and began hacking at the base of the well. His face was fierce as he labored, as if God would seriously take offense. After a moment he leaned thoughtfully on his shovel. "This may not actually qualify as *avodah*—forbidden. Because I'm destroying as I work, not creating."

"Destroying in order to create your thesis."

"Just so," he said, and resumed digging. I felt bad for him; it didn't take Freud to see he was disturbed. His shovel flailing, his breath coming hard, I became concerned for his health. Any mishap or heart attack sustained on my land could leave me liable.

His students returned down the embankment. Up close they looked frightfully young; my conceit of eternal boyishness took a beating in comparison. Doubtless I seemed a yuppie fart to them, or, worse, some kind of role model. To prove myself a regular guy I launched some wit at Jill the landscaper's daughter. "Gershom," I winked, "is defying the Lord. He'll be done in a minute."

Jill resembled a Native American in her coloring and vengeful stare. I have great respect for Indians; the way they're exploiting uranium deposits and casino gambling on their reservations in order to get back in the upward-mobility game has my total support. "It's not your place to mock our teacher," Jill chided me.

"You're right. I'm sorry." Another latent maternal type, I thought—Gershom her papoose.

Meanwhile his shovel had started clanging on impact where before it had smoothly scooped. He'd dug a foot deeper than the well's former bottom. He paused. "So that's why the welldigger stopped digging. He dug all this way down only to hit granite." Gershom scraped away dirt with the shovel to reveal gray rock beneath, scarred white where the shovel had struck it.

"Tough luck," I said.

"For both of you. Must be all ledge under here. To finish leveling this area, you're going to have to blast."

"Oh no," Jill said. When someone asked if blasting was bad, she answered, "Not bad. Expensive."

"Didn't he know?"

"He didn't know."

"Hey! My excavator gave me a set price. Any extra's on him."

"There was no clause in his contract about rock or ground water?" Jill asked me. "It's pretty standard."

"Standard" rang a bell. I remembered my attorney saying it as he highlighted a line in the contract. I swallowed. "How much will it cost me, do you think?"

"No way to know till they do it. They measure—"

"Don't tell me. By the yard."

Jill nodded. I had a mental image of her writhing in pagan ecstacy, singing chants for my soul—the shock of lost money had made me feverish. She said, "My dad always figures $2,000 a day, for blasting. He jokes that they never take less than four days, no matter how small the job."

"Funny guy."

"Four, times two thousand—" Gershom began.

"I know, goddamn it!" I toed the exposed rock. "Pity it wasn't gold."

"Not your day, old sport."

Jill Eagle-Eye knelt to Gershom's dirt pile and extracted a crudded coin. She spat on it, a primitive girl, and cleaned it with her shirt. "A penny," she smiled, handing it to me.

"1943. Hell, I thought it'd be colonial-era, at least."

Gershom said, "Circa World War II corresponds to when I estimated this neighborhood to have been settled. It's nice to be proved right. The coin must have fallen out of the guy's pocket while he was digging."

"He made a wish!" Jill said. "Where's your sense of romance, Gershom? I bet he wished for world peace."

"I bet he wished for water," I said. As I started to throw the coin away, Gershom grabbed my arm:

"It may be worth something."

"Twenty bucks? Thirty? I have my pride."

Jill said, "I'll take it, if you don't want it. I think it's kind of mysterious."

I gave her the coin. My Indian hallucination was now out of control, raging through me like smallpox. In the lines of her palm I saw centuries of free love; in her eyes I saw campfires, me sprawled before them, bound and naked as this brown-skinned maid adored my palest parts. Jill's fingers gripped my wampum.

"A penny for my thoughts?" she joked.

"Better yours than mine."

Gershom said, "Tell me, is it copper?"

"Pennies usually are."

She scratched it with a fingernail. "Copper it is. Okay?"

"That's fine."

The students had found nothing interesting. They wanted to go to a bar, catch the end of the Red Sox game. Gershom agreed. I apologized that my well had flopped. "I didn't expect much," he confessed. "This area's fairly static. But when Susan called me, I couldn't resist." He got into his truck.

"Mind if I tag along?"

"With us? You serious?"

"I love baseball. And my TV's broken." My TV was fine and I hate baseball. The game is all situation, all wondering and waiting. I get enough of that in the day-to-day without sitting down to watch it.

"How can I say no?" He smiled—and fell right into my trap.

Following in my car, I refined my plan. I must inspire

Gershom to fight for his wife, must prove myself to be such utter scum as to compel him, by his duties as a husband and citizen, to deliver her from my destructive attentions and deliver me from hers. I'd never broken up with someone before; I feared a tedious scene. Too, I was sure Susan would dump me any day now, without a tear. I liked my plan better.

The tricky part was nauseating Gershom while at the same time charming Jill, for I wanted Susan out of my life and this Arapaho maiden in it. Divide and conquer being the objective, when Jill ordered a beer from the waitress and Gershom a club soda, I, not usually a drinker, ordered a beer and a bourbon chaser, hoping to connect with her and alienate Gershom. This was my plan. Even today I believe it could have worked.

I remember realizing at some point that I was drunk and no one else was even tipsy. To rectify this, I ordered daiquiris by the pitcher and forced them on my companions. Jill several times asked me to stop calling her Little Wing. I agreed in exchange for a dance—to a baseball game, which is easier than you might think. Gershom was a ghost on the periphery of my blurred perception. I didn't try to salvage my plan till after I vomited. Once purged, however, I was newly cognizant. I asked Gershom to drive me home—or better, that he and Jill drive me home, for I recognized Gershom as a man immune to humiliation unless before witnesses.

At first Jill refused to come. But when I refused to leave without her, her friends demanded she reconsider. All was settled except the bill. I discovered I had no money. "Only plastique," I gurgled to the waitress.

"We don't take credit cards here."

On the table were daiquiri pitchers, beer bottles, and some empty shot glasses by me. No one had wanted this many drinks, so I'd promised I would pay. "You'll take a personal check?"

"Local?" the waitress said. "I guess so."

"Excellent." With her pen in my fist I paid the tab and a massive tip. Everyone thanked me for my generosity, except Jill, who held out with charming petulance.

"What is this crap!" The waitress read from the check I'd

handed her: "Not valid for less than five hundred dollars."

"Lemme see." It appeared I'd brought the wrong check-book. "It's funny, really. This is from a money fund. It's—"

"No good."

"For five hundred, sure it is. Got change?"

She stared at me.

I shrugged to my companions. "Okay, folks. Ante up." Wordlessly they emptied their pockets. A meager pile of bills and coins collected at the center of the table. Gershom counted it.

"We're good," he said.

I protested, "A little light on the tip."

"That's all there is, Philip! We're broke."

"Okay. Fine. She's lucky to get it." I laboriously noted everyone's address on a napkin so I could reimburse them by mail. Jill said send her money care of Gershom. I offered my goodbyes and the three of us departed. Only later did I realize I'd left the napkin with the names on the table.

In Gershom's pickup I squeezed between Gershom and Jill.

"A truck-driving Jew is rare," I observed. "A Jew in a Mercedes, that's different. Very common. Your father drives a Mercedes."

Gershom was silent a moment. "Yes he does."

"Nothing wrong with that. Let bygones be bygones, I say. Though there is a certain irony—"

He cut me off. "If you're going to make reference to Nazis and the Holocaust, don't use the word irony. It does not apply."

"I'm speaking of Jews in German luxury cars, Gershom. As for the Holocaust—"

"Please. It offends me. You offend me."

"I understand. But for the record, I too think genocide is bad."

"Good God."

"A Ford-driving Jew?" I continued, referring to the make of his truck. "Also ironic. Because Henry the First was mucho anti-Semitic. I swear, sometimes it seems there's nowhere to run."

"If you can't beat 'em, join 'em," he said pointedly. He was proud of that one, was Gershom.

85

I gave him directions to Chinaland, my restaurant-home. A sharp turn thrust me against Jill. I surreptitiously sniffed her, detecting sagebrush and woodsmoke. Indians have no personal scent; this is due to a lack of body hair, itself an enchanting attribute. With somnolence beginning to overwhelm me, I skipped the small talk: "Go out with me. Take a chance."

She ignored me.

I sighed, "I have money but no one to share it with." Girls dig self-mockery.

"You are not my type."

"What *is* your type? I'll adapt. I can teach or be taught, these are my gifts to you."

"What happened to money?" Gershom broke in. His voice was jokey and meant for Jill.

"Who needs it?" she said at me, to him. "I'm a hippie at heart."

"Love is all you need?" he asked.

"Love is all."

Their banter excluded me, which was Gershom's intent. His intrusion in my suave seduction was his way of rescuing Jill. It was an act of friendship on his part, but in my impaired state I thought he was stealing my action. "Don't bother with Gersh," I told her. "He couldn't satisfy his wife, much less a love savage like yourself."

She recoiled as from fumes.

"Have you met Susan?" I pressed. "Some might deem her a sexual freak, but I think she's neat."

Gershom slammed the brakes. My spine, alcoholically rubberized, slung me face first into the dashboard. I tasted blood and the pain was severe. "You broke by dose!"

"You broke it yourself."

"Be! You hit the brakes."

"Goodbye, Philip. You're home."

"Chida-ladd?"

"Yes. Now out."

I turned to Jill. "By dose, it looks bad?"

"It looks bigger."

"Big dose, big dick. Could it be? Yes it could." Sensing

that ribaldry would get me nowhere, I issued a straightforward plea: "Walk be up?"

"To your apartment? Get real."

"I'll walk you up," Gershom said. "Wouldn't want you to get mugged." He assisted me upstairs. On the way, I asked him Jill's last name. "MacDougal," he said.

"A Scot! Begorrah. So am I."

"I thought you said you were Jewish."

"I lied. I'm nothing, remember?" I bent to my doorknob and sighted the key to the keyhole. "Scottish," I marveled. "A comely bitch, too."

Gershom kicked me. Soccer style, swinging up from my right rear quarter into my solar plexus. I dropped like a laundry sack and went fetal and silent until my breathing resumed with farm animal sounds, moos and bleats and finally dry heaves, my poor belly with nothing to offer but traces of bile and beer nuts. I studied the boot that had felled me, a Timberland. It launched at my sternum. More moans, more mating calls. I spoke to the boot: "No fair."

Gershom's voice sounded stern and unwelcome far above me, like God's in the ears of Adam. "I've wanted to do that all day, you son of a bitch. I'm sure I'll regret it later."

"Why wait?"

"You're disgusting."

"You're short."

"With you, my wife has outdone herself."

I rolled on my back. "There were others?"

He laughed. "Disgusting and vain. Yes, there were others—you are but one in a sorry progression." Shaking his head, he started away.

Clearly we'd come to a crossroads in our acquaintance, an opportunity for a fresh start. I could have begged him to think better of me, groveled before him in pathetic apology and maudlin self-laceration. I stuck with my original plan instead, a plan originating perhaps three years, not three hours, ago, of digging myself an interesting grave. "Don't forget your history," I called after him. "You couldn't keep your wife, old sport. You didn't have the stuff!"

Gershom returned, stood now over me. I touched my finger to my tongue and scored one for the bad guys. He nodded his head jerkily, answering inner voices. I saw what was coming. Observing Frank Bakes six days earlier, I'd become familiar with one way love transmogrifies, when lovers revert to their essential form as tyrants of dependency or as glacial, unreachable brats. So when Gershom spat on me I didn't flinch. As with Frank Bakes, Gershom's imitation of biblical scorn was the last resort of a beaten man. Unlike Frank, however, Gershom didn't let fly in exuberant loathing, but rather oozed a long looey that dropped from its strand like a slow forlorn teardrop and splatted below my eye, sliding silkenly into my ear. Many witticisms occurred to me. I said nothing. I felt sad for him. The guy had nothing left.

Conversation was pretty much killed between us. My last sight of him was the back of his head, his yarmulke sinking down the drab stairwell like a sunset seen through smog.

The linoleum floor of the hallway was comfortable to lie on. I fell asleep. A stranger woke me, a Ho Chi Minh lookalike with gray wisps on his chin and teeth like little black pearls. He helped me to my feet, wiping saliva and grime from my face with his handkerchief. Those black teeth identified him as an opium user. I wondered if he could spare me some to ease my aches and pains. "Got smackee?" I asked. But junkies never share.

How I hurt! Belly and breastbone for starters, a mouth that felt sandblasted and a nose that felt bigger. The Chinese man unlocked my door for me, then shuffled down the hall. Outside his apartment he turned and waved jauntily. I waved back. It's good to know one's neighbors.

I showered, put on my bathrobe, somehow wound up on the floor again, passed out on my back. I opened my eyes to see Carrie Donley standing upside down in my doorway. "Surprise! You left your key in the lock."

From the floor I said, "I thought our arrangement was to always phone ahead."

"Timmy surprised me by bringing me to this restaurant." She was swaying, a bit sauced herself.

"Timmy is here, you say?" My head pounded.

"Downstairs. With his mom and my folks. It's patch-up-the-marriage time, four against one. They ambushed me."

"I advise surrender. I could never honestly care for you." This candor passed my lips like the eager recitation of abject repentence I expect to speak on my deathbed.

Her response was unfazed. "Except I want you, kid. They think I'm in the ladies' room."

"You're mad at them, so you want to fuck me."

"Don't analyze, Philly. *Do.*" She loomed above me, straddling my hips.

"I'm really not able. I've been drinking."

Carrie's expression turned thoughtful. Brightening, she raised her skirt and knelt over my head, her open thighs veiling me like moist nightfall in a tropical jungle. I'd already trekked many miles today. No rest for the weary, however.

She called the next morning to apologize for her behavior.

"You used me," I said.

"Was it awful?"

"Only if photographed."

Carrie giggled. "Aw Philly, I'm gonna miss you." The way she then ended our affair was a model of candor and clarity. Doing it on the phone was a masterstroke, especially after last night's encounter, a sex act so archetypal it summed us up like an epilogue. I would have liked to dismiss Susan likewise, on the phone with fond regret. But just as I hung up on Carrie, Susan telephoned me, ruining my timing.

"How did it go with Gershom yesterday?"

"Oh swell."

"He said so, too. He had a message for you, about Jill Somebody and a coin you gave her?"

"Go on."

"He made me write it down. '1943 copper penny. Copper shortage during war, most pennies steel. Copper rare, very' underlined 'valuable. Jill says thanks.' You gave her this coin?"

"The details are hazy."

"It's really rare, apparently. You should get it back."

"And be an Indian giver?"

"Why is that funny?" When I quit laughing, she asked me to come to her office tomorrow. "It's time to talk."

"About our relationship? The phone is fine, I'm used to it."

"The phone is bullshit! See you tomorrow."

Neil was with her when I entered Gray Realtors. I recalled Gershom's suspicions about his father's infatuation with Susan, but seeing them together now, it didn't fit. Still, they seemed allied in something by the way they glowered at me. I took the offensive. "You screwed me, Neil. I got ledge under my property." That morning, my foreman had told me four days' blasting should clear it. I'd brought up the pilfered topsoil. Okay, two days.

Neil said, "I didn't know. And if I did, so what? I don't run a charity."

"Did you or didn't you? I'm curious."

"Number one, I don't like you. Number two, no. Ask me if I care."

"Both of you shut up," Susan said.

"Why doesn't he like me?" I asked. "What did I do to him?"

"Not to me," Neil said. "Her."

I paused to assess. Her I'd done things to.

"I'm pregnant," Susan said.

"By me?"

"I'll ignore that."

"We're gonna have a baby," Neil said.

"We?"

"Yeah. Me and Susie. She's not alone in this." He put his arm around her and hugged her to him, *hugged* her. Gershom was right! The man was a monster! I yanked her away from him.

"That's my ladyfriend, pal!"

"Oh, get off it! You don't want a baby. You know you don't."

"Hah! I do *not* know I don't."

Susan said, "Do you, Philip? I thought no way."

Neil was ranting, "He don't phone, he don't stop by—"

"Hush." She awaited my answer. I stalled:

"Do I want it? The baby, you mean."

"Yes, the baby. Our baby."

"Sure I do. Absolutely."

"The truth, Philip. It's all right."

"I want the goddamn baby!" And I didn't want Neil to get it, the filthy lech.

"I'd have it regardless. But if you want to take part . . ."

"What about Gershom? He matters here."

"We're getting divorced. That's why he phoned me yesterday, to tell me he's filing. I'm surprised he took the step. Did you encourage him?"

Words failed me. On Neil's desk a letter opener looked right for hari-kari. "It's for the best," Neil was saying. "He needs to grow up."

"If you think *you're* moving in, forget it. Stay away from my fiancé!"

Susan laughed. "I'm not marrying you."

"Our child a bastard?"

"Don't be a fool. I barely know you. I barely like you."

"In time."

"What'd I tell you?" Neil said to her. "If we'd kept quiet, he woulda taken himself outta the picture. I know his type."

"And I know yours! Disgusting you are, and a newlywed to boot!"

"What is he saying? I don't understand what he's saying. He's worse than Gerald."

"Your son's name is *Gershom*," I shouted. "Get it right!"

"Hey all! Lookit what I bought!" A woman flounced through the office door and hurtled toward us, bearing boxes and bags before her like a cannonball shot through a clothing store. Red of lip, impossibly blond, when she set down her packages there were fewer than I'd thought, for much of what she carried was her, gifts upon gifts, you could say. She kissed Neil, "Hey lover," kissed Susan, "Hey mom," and gave me a knowing wink. "Hey stud."

Neil sighed. "Philip. My wife Dominique."

Oh, that first impression! She was a weatherfront raising the temperature, a ship's figurehead sailing tits first. She dispelled with one stroke all of my suspicions about Neil. For no man, leastwise none as clever as he, could be unhappy with a wench like Dominique. Because no man marries such an awesome stereotype intending to be happy. Happy is a long shot, happy takes work. He marries her to become merely happi*er*.

Gershom, I thought—you lied!

In her packages were receiving blankets and assorted infant outfits. "There's the neatest baby shop right down the street. They have nursery furniture, Italian. The best. Christ, Susie," Dominique beamed. "I'm walking on air. If you don't name me godmother, I swear I'll strangle you. And I babysit for free."

"It's too soon to buy stuff. I don't want to jinx it."

"Fooey. Let's have fun with it. Let's get fat together."

"You'll move into our house," Neil said to Susan. "We'll give you the guest wing."

"Separate entrance," Dominique said. "Your own space. Gentleman callers out by ten. Just kidding," she said to me.

I was confused. Susan took my hand and led me toward the privacy of the conference room. Dominique stepped up:

"Phil. I wanna say something. People been telling me you're the biggest butthole going. I don't listen. When I married Neil, I brought some hurt on this family, but thanks to you we're gonna come out of it. I just know we are, I can feel it." She kissed me. Not as young as Susan had implied, she was maybe forty-five, an age along with fourteen or fifteen that is surely a woman's prime.

"I'm confused," I said.

In the conference room Susan explained, though I'd guessed as much, that Gershom and Dominique didn't get along. Dominique's offense, in Gershom's mind, was being Neil's first serious love since the death of Neil's wife, Gershom's mother. Ostensibly, however, it was Dominique's telling of a joke about Jews and avarice that Gershom wouldn't forgive—the family had fractured subsequently. Susan explained to me that she and Gershom had been unable to conceive a child; and that Neil, resentful of Gershom's snub of Dominique, had made harsh reference to his son's somewhat meager sperm count. In fact the fertility problem lay with Susan, the result of an ectopic pregnancy years earlier that had cost her one Fallopian tube. "My chances of getting pregnant again were almost nil. Don't ask me how," she said, fiddling with my shirt buttons, "but somehow you broke through."

"My miracle seed."

She laid her head on my chest; a gesture that was, despite countless comminglings of psyches and body fluids, a first in our relationship. "You said it," she said.

I asked her to marry me.

She raised her head and stepped away, not panicked or angry but sadly stern. "No."

"How bad could it be?"

"I'd rather be friends. For the baby's sake."

"No making love?"

"Was that what it was? It felt like war."

"Whatever works."

She shook her head. "Just friends."

Friends? With Susan? No more little lady down on all fours to tongue my fingers and fly? It was too strange. "A question," I said. "Did you have affairs during your marriage, before me?" She looked at me sidelong, tightly coiling under the blow of my comment like a snake reacting to danger. "Not because of the baby," I said quickly. "I'm asking for myself."

She hesitated only an instant. "You're it."

"Why me?"

"Right time, right place." Her face softened. "Right guy."

She may have been lying, but in truth I didn't really care to know other intimate facts of her marriage. I needed a reason, even one soiled with condescension, to believe I wasn't all bad.

So Susan and I were lovers no more. It was the escape I'd wanted, and yet, now that it had come to pass, kind of what I didn't want. I looked at the bright side. It was early, she was new with child—I had time to persuade her to snuff it. Then we could scrap the friend baloney and get back to whatever works.

Fathers-to-be often speak of pregnancy's unreality—certainly in the beginning, but sometimes even in the last trimester when the swallowed pumpkin swells and spins with such alarming verity it seems surely fabricated, a movie special effect. Most befuddled is the man who from week one steadies his spouse on the slightest inclines, fetches her plate at picnics, hassles her obstetrician and obsesses about layette. I refrained from such displays. Nor did I go the other way and behave as if nothing was changed, say, blowing smoke in my woman's face and teasing her with fat jokes. Susan's pregnancy was real to me, neither thrilling nor intimidating. I took it in stride.

We were friends now, and as friends do, we lunched together once a week. Sometimes in the restaurant she'd press my hand to her belly and let me feel the curve; I'd picture the lurid sex we shared as around us restaurant patrons nudged each other at the sight of such a darling couple. Regarding sex, I was back to getting none. Susan was completely uninterested. She kept our conversation to matters of her health, the baby's, her ongoing divorce. I listened and smiled and drowned my irritation in many midday cocktails. Even early in her pregnancy her breasts seemed bigger to me, her features more sensual. When the drinks took hold I invariably offered her money for doctor bills, maternity clothes, which she invariably refused. She was still working at the realty office, she said, and Neil offered an insurance plan that covered maternity costs. In fact, the plan's benefits came mostly out Neil's wallet—he was wedging himself between Susan and me by playing the big provider. But I was in no position to compete. For the first time ever, more money was flowing out of my accounts than flowed in.

With the new building and girl trouble and a baby on the way, I'd taken my eye off the stock market. Incredibly, it had become unreal to me. The numbers on my Quotron screen confused and mocked me, like babble in the ears of a linguist. Good news meant nothing; bad news I received with punch-drunken numbness, feeling the blows only later. To regain lost poise I pared my life of distraction. I cut down on lunches with Susan. Seeing her every few weeks gave her pregnancy a time-lapse vividness. But rather than make me want to get closer to her, her burgeoning condition encouraged my disinterest. So changed was she each time we met, I scarcely recognized her. She was eclipsed somehow, a functionary of the fetus she carried. Her complaints of weight-gain and discomfort seemed less characteristically bitchy than a glad lending of her voice to the whining choir of young mothers everywhere. Even remembering and wanting the sex we'd had began to bring me waves of nausea such as a pervert might feel at home on Mother's Day. Our common ground had been rezoned. She was as strange to me as the thing inside her.

Meanwhile, work proceeded slowly on the building. It stayed empty, unleased. Nick's Pizza had vacated before construction began, and Melina's Little Bud Shop couldn't take occupancy until a million code violations were rectified. I was operating at a deficit, which I carried only by borrowing against my stocks at an interest rate that had recently risen. The stocks themselves were no joy either. I'd got caught in a technology correction and in the infamous video game crash of 1983. Apple, Coleco, Warner Communications all tumbled as one; to cover margin calls I sold my Ellis and my Pervis-Glastrop, stocks dear to me since childhood. To save money I discontinued my Quotron service. I'd increasingly been using the brokerage's facilities; still it was a wrenching moment when they carted my unit away.

I looked good, however. The clothing I'd bought as part of my makeover was high quality. I did make the mistake of buying all-cotton shirts, thus couldn't use the laundromat. Dry cleaning bills were thorns in my budget; I minimized these by recycling my shirts through several wearings, smothering any unfortunate odors with a hefty splash of Polo cologne. Macaroni and cheese was my usual fare. My Chinese neighbor sometimes ordered takeout from the restaurant downstairs; the food cartons he left outside his door provided me decent pickings. I pawned my old earring. To save on razors I grew a goatee, which made a dapper match with my Italian suits. I sold my car and rode city buses thereafter, me with my cashmere topcoat and alligator briefcase heading downtown with black maids and janitors. My assets were in the hundreds of thousands, but that niggling negative cash flow was a sword above my head. If not an absolute necessity, my austere lifestyle was prudent. A similar argument applies to my partnership with Peter Rice, the office manager at the brokerage. His proposal of an insider trading scheme was distasteful yet tempting. My head said no but my heart said yes, a new kind of conflict for me.

"Insider trading scheme"—I use the generic description to avoid any misunderstanding. I broke the law. I became Peter's personal portfolio manager, trading through an outside account of which, like a good company man, he was a blind beneficiary. For pay I took a standard percentage of his monthly yield, augmented by profits in my own accounts derived from the very same trades. Peter supplied the information and I took appropriate action. The arrangement made me more money than it did him, yet kept me his subordinate in our two-man hierarchy, thereby meeting each other's criterion for trust and peace of mind. I had no knowledge of his source. He said he didn't know the person either. "We deal in code. He's Bluebird Two when I phone him." I asked Peter, "Are you Bluebird One?" "What did I tell you, Phil? No questions." Later, I learned Bluebird Two was a washroom attendant in a Wall Street law firm, a cocaine dealer who accepted stock tips in lieu of cash. I think Peter was embarrassed that our enterprise was rooted in something as common as drug dealing; certainly to my mind it took the gloss off what had seemed a neat idea. It's a question of aesthetics such as distinguishes an art thief from a purse snatcher, a bigamist from a child molester. I felt dirty when I learned the truth.

We made a lot of money very fast. Get his tip, buy the option, rake in the dough: easy. It was a sleepwalk with no memory at waking. Ask me how, exactly, I made $600,000 in six months and I can only shrug. I remember something about Gulf Oil and T. Boone Pickens, something about Beatrice. It's someone else's dream beyond that.

My biggest benefit was sleeping at night. Operating in the red during the preceding months, I'd been plagued with insomnia to such a degree I wondered if poor people ever slept; solvency brought back to me the eight unburdened hours of rest I need to maintain optimism. And I was able finally to complete renovations on the building. With pride I inspected my expanded parking lot, the sidewalk with its handicap ramp, the tiled bathrooms and noiseless low-profile commodes; trading only stocks and bonds, I'd never known the satisfaction of creating something real. I spent little of the money I was making on myself. I stayed with my apartment and with public transportation. I'm not one to live high on ill-gotten gains. I tend toward guilt and bitter self-judgment, though I always suspend the sentence.

I rented the upstairs floor of the building to two dentists. Melina's Little Bud Shop occupied the first-floor retail space. Nick's mother, old Mrs. Bakes, ran the cash register with the stolid intensity of a crane operator, casting her lot with Nick instead of her elder son Frank.

Poor Frank. He had loser written all over him when I ran into him in December, at the brokerage of all places. There, in a sullen hulk at the end of the lobby bench, was the drunken anti-Semite himself, a private investor now. My goatee threw him at first; recognizing me, he seemed glad to see me, truly a lonesome fellow. In the manner of most newly reformed, it took about a minute for him to lay his life nakedly open to me. He was in Alcoholics Anonymous, he was a follower of Jesus Christ, and he was getting murdered in the stock market. "That's rough," I sympathized. To fill the silence I asked if he'd seen the new, improved building.

"I watch yesterday," he said.

"Watch?"

"I watch Melina and Nikos and our mother. In my car I watch them all day with the damn flowers."

"That doesn't sound too healthy, Frank."

"I was too shamed to visit. They make the money like fists, and I do piss in the ocean. I drive away finally."

"Money isn't everything. I'm sure they would have loved to see you."

"Without my pride, Philly, I cannot do this. I must be standing big like them. Then I can say I forgive."

"And making money will return your pride?"

"My investing! My American capital dream! But so far is shit. Every stock I buy falls like a dead bird."

"Who's your broker?"

"Myself."

There was a time when I'd believed that achieving success was the first step toward establishing parity with one's enemy. Father had been my enemy, once. But wealthy in my own right now, I'd realized that financial success would no more persuade him of my worth than it persuaded me. I was ready to reconcile with him. The suspense of our estrangement had begun to weigh on me. Would it end with welcome-home hugs or with somebody's death? I wanted to know; I wanted, as attorneys say, to bring the matter to closure. Unable to effect a reconciliation for real, I resolved to do it vicariously, through Frank. I'd make Frank rich, then take heart as triumphantly he entered Melina's Little Bud Shop and forgave those who'd sinned against him. I told him to open an account with Timmy Donley, "one of the brokers here."

"He's a sharpie?"

"He's a dummy. But trust me."

Matching his stock trades with my own, I'd made Frank Bakes quite well-off by March 1984. Timmy had been earning commissions hand over fist on my business alone; now with Frank's commissions included, it was getting obscene. Timmy got smug. I didn't mind him strutting like a rooster ever since Carrie came back to him. I didn't mind that his clients were copying my trades exactly or even that Timmy was participating, buying a Toyota and a Rolex with the profits. But when, one day, while leaving for lunch with some office colleagues, he walked by me in the brokerage lobby without acknowledging my greeting, I knew it was time to discipline him.

Timmy's mother had told me he was being considered for

promotion to the head office in New York. My first idea was to let it happen, let Timmy show his true stuff in a job he could never have managed. My affection for Thelma dissuaded me from orchestrating such a public comeuppance. Instead, I took Timmy aside and gently reminded him that he was a no-talent clerk, I was his master and benefactor, and that any more snotty displays of ingratitude would be to his eternal regret. I was shocked when he said to go fuck myself.

I wondered if his impertinence came of more than inflated ego. I phoned his wife Carrie, after six months of silence, to see if in some fit of candor she'd told him of our affair. Timmy had access to my private business—I had to know if I could trust him. She said she had not. I next asked if she thought about us ever. She said she did. "Really?" I said. "Like how?"

Ever since Carrie broke off with me, I'd been haunted by nighttime visions of her, masturbatory holograms conjured to cure wakefulness; those visions took a sugary turn the very night after I contacted her again. Rather than the madcap antics of a jolly dominatrix, I now imagined her lying in bed beside me, the two of us naked and facing front to front with the room lights on—talking, if you can believe it, about our kids in school and her job and mine and whose parents we'd endure next holiday. I attribute my deviance to Susan, whom I was losing to her domestic dream. To compensate, I was casting Carrie in a similar dream of my own. Perhaps it was pre-dictable that my life's next pitfall should come disguised as a happy home.

When Carrie and I met the next day for an afternoon drink, I could barely brag of my business success for the crazy voices in my head demanding instant conformity: "Ask her to marry you! Take her grocery shopping! Copulate in the missionary style and kiss her when you come!"

Across the table, Carrie wore a lovely sad expression. "I'm married," she said, cutting short the jabber in my head and mouth. "I'm married but I desire you. Which means I shouldn't be married." She looked at me. "You were the last person I needed to hear from. I'd almost fooled myself."

"Into thinking you didn't like me?"

She grew quizzical. "How old are you, Philip?"

At this irrelevancy, the voices in my head went haywire with impatience: "Ask her to copulate! Take her to the missionary! Kiss her in the married style and come when you grocery shop!" I stammered, "Twenty-four."

"I'm almost twenty-seven. So when do we drop 'like' for 'love'? When do we upgrade the language? I'm asking because I don't know."

"Some people say 'love' from the start. Some refrain."

"As early as high school, Timmy was saying he loved me—and my feelings for him faded. You never got sentimental with me at all, and I can't stop thinking about you."

"I've thought about you a lot, too." I described the vision I'd had of her. "We're lying together uncovered in bed. Chatting. Nuzzling. Exchanging views."

"Like old people? That's beautiful." Then she said, "I've had visions, too. Of you and me holding hands."

"Like kids?"

"Just like kids."

I reached across the table and took her hand in mine. "It's a start." She leaned down and pressed her cheek to my wrist.

"I missed you, you prick." Then, with a tone that progressed from sheep to wolf, "I've had other visions, too."

We were in bed twenty minutes later. Before we got serious, I arranged us like I'd pictured it in my mind. The electric light was harsh on our physical imperfections, but that was the point, I think. Our fingers entwined with a sort of fearful delicacy, like the palps of courting crustaceans.

"Philly," she said. "That thing on your face—"

"My goatee? Kinda cool, huh?"

"You look like an idiot. Shave it."

I put on a baby voice. "Do I hafta?"

She smiled. Sexual tics are like riding a bicycle—you never forget. "Oh you naughty boy . . ."

Later we talked. She pondered leaving Timmy, filing for divorce, moving in with me. I cut her off with regret. I had to get downtown to the hospital to meet Susan for our Lamaze class. It had almost slipped my mind.

Of my many missteps in those pivotal weeks, participating with Susan in her Lamaze instruction was the biggest. I wasn't needed. There was a lesbian in our class whose girlfriend was her breathing coach (the lesbian had been artificially inseminated, she explained to us all. "Me too," Susan said), and it struck me that Alison or Dominique could have managed the chore for Susan. The prospect of attending the birth didn't worry me; I have high tolerance for other people's pain. But I was skittish about getting attached to the baby during preparations for its arrival. It had grown conveniently remote from me with each interval of noncontact with its mother. And since seeing Susan less, my material fortunes had soared. I was superstitious about altering the balance.

She insisted. Despite her tough talk about having and supporting the child alone, she wanted a partner to give the process normalcy. The nearer her due date, the crankier she became. It was her old manner again, vulnerability countered with punitive measures, though this time its cause wasn't her embarrassing (to her) sexual submissiveness, but rather, to quote Susan, "the goddamn kid and its asshole father." I was drawn to the baby as a fellow conspirator. When, during our second Lamaze class, she cussed the baby while huffing through her exercises, I kissed her basketball belly and said, "Don't talk to my child that way!" Susan's eyes flared combatively. Then she smiled. What she wanted, I think she realized at that moment, was the natural bond of a mother and father and child, the bond most people achieve without trying. All her good sense was against it. All emotion in favor.

Carrie had abandoned Timmy and was holed up at a friend's place waiting for me to marry her. Not for love or because I'm so great, but because at the time her mind was more muddled than mine; she even forgot to resume birth control after she left her husband. I didn't believe it either. I believed she'd got herself pregnant to lock us together first as parents and then as man and wife. And I probably would have fallen for it had I not just been through it with Susan. I wouldn't be bullied this time. I quickly wore down Carrie's delusions of motherhood, even had her agreeing that abortion was in everyone's interest, not least the baby's.

Timmy, dumped again, didn't fall into the weepy depression that had followed their earlier split. He was downright snide in the last of our business dealings, acting as if I had no cause to transfer my portfolio to another brokerage when it was his own inflated self-importance that was forcing me to do it. Finally I said, "It's business, Timmy. We had a nice ride, now it's over. You must seek your fortune alone."

"Good riddance, Phil."

With sadness I realized the kindly pothead I'd known in college was dead. I'd created a monster. "Don't be an ingrate, Timmy. I made you a lot of money."

"You? Or Peter Rice?"

Created a monster indeed—with power to kill its creator!

He grinned, watching my reaction. "Don't worry, Phil. I'm just as guilty as you, for letting these dirty deals happen. For taking advantage."

"And don't you forget it."

Thelma Donley and Frank Bakes were on the bench in the outside lobby. Frank had become a regular here, watching his wealth replicate with the glee of a kid breeding hamsters. I wasn't keen on seeing Thelma, thinking Timmy might have turned her against me. Frank hollered me over: "You Philly! Come see something!" He and Thelma had started dating and evidently had got serious. He lifted her hand to show me her emerald ring.

"Congratulations. What'd you do, Frank, hit the number?"

He gave me a wink. "My stocks are killer. I don't know why."

"It's your broker," Thelma said. She knew nothing, bless her. "My Timmy is a genius."

Frank said to me, "Tomorrow I go with Telma to the flower shop. We get new Cadillac in morning and so Melina and Nikos will see how I am success. *And* with a hot woman!" Thelma laid her head on his shoulder. "I will forgive them, Philly. I am ten times their shit now. I owe this to you."

"You mean Timmy," Thelma corrected him.

"Of course." He winked again. "Teemy!"

That night I met Susan for our third Lamaze class. I still had no car, so bused to the hospital where the classes were held. The instructor guided our group, as integrated as Sesame Street, through the birthing rooms and maternity ward. We saw some babies behind a big window that was like an aquarium wall, the newborn babies like larval sea creatures, sleeping and crying in a sort of dense silence. Susan took my hand as we watched. I thought of Carrie; her abortion was scheduled for tomorrow. I hoped she wasn't alone on this eve, but better alone than here, seeing these. I felt like a dispassionate angel watching lives on earth unfold simultaneously, Susan's and Carrie's and babies' born and unborn. It was a lousy feeling—so exhausting knowing the future. The maternity ward was warm and my hand in Susan's sweated. She didn't seem to mind. We were intimates for better or worse, for now.

She was due in four weeks. And though clearly her heart had softened toward me, she still mingled need with autocratic standoffishness in her bid to be superwoman. Nothing captured her contradictions more than when, over coffee after that third Lamaze class (hers decaf, mine Irish), she gave me a telephone beeper to wear, with instructions to call her whenever it beeped. "It'll mean my contractions have started. You drive to Neil's house, pick me up, and we'll go have this kid. But call first, so I'll know you're on the way."

"I thought we could meet at the hospital."

"You want me to drive myself? I'll only be in agony. Maybe I should hitchhike. Maybe I should jog."

"Maybe Neil could drive you, since you're living there."

"The father of my child can't be bothered?"

"I don't have a car, is the problem."

"I told you to buy one!" True; and it was a command I'd gladly obeyed. Public transportation had lost its charm for me. "I've ordered a BMW. I take delivery in two months."

"I take delivery in one! You rent something, goddamn it. I could pop any minute."

I finished my coffee. "They do have a Porsche for lease."

103

Susan wanted to test the beeper. She went to the pay phone and dialed the call numbers. On the table the beeper beeped in squeaky bursts like a burglar alarm in Lilliput. I've since heard that sound in nightmares.

When I got back to my place I telephoned Carrie. "All set for tomorrow?"

"Oh sure."

"You'll pick me up when?" Since I had no car, we'd planned for Carrie to drive to my place. Then I would take over so she could relax on the ride to and from the abortion clinic.

"Five o'clock. They're open late Fridays." She gave a hard laugh. "Like a bank."

"It's for the best, Carrie. We're not fit to be parents together."

"It goes against everything I believe in. For other people, I think abortion is their own private business. For me, I think it's wrong. It's murder," she said, her voice cracking.

"A *little* murder."

"Whatsat mean?"

"You pull a garden seedling, it's a little murder. You chop down a sequoia, it's heinous." I'd given the matter some thought, knowing Carrie would want comfort. "It's like in geometry, a point as compared to a line. A point has no dimension. It has no past or future. In itself it doesn't exist."

"A baby has a future."

"A six-week-old fetus does not."

"It could!"

"Its future belongs to you. It's your choice."

She took time to consider. "I *am* barely pregnant."

"Exactly. It's one life at this point. *Yours.* Take charge of it." This last was a low blow—an inability to take charge of her life was the source of Carrie's insecurity. Her self-esteem had grown immensely since when we'd first become lovers. My having now to destroy it was no cause for satisfaction, as once it might have been.

"You're right. No one's gonna drag me down, not even a baby."

"Atta girl."

"Philly?"

"Yes?"

She hesitated. Her voice was meek, completely regressed into helplessness. "What will we be, after tomorrow? Will we be lovers or friends or what?"

"We'll be allies, Carrie."

"That sounds okay."

"I agree."

"And Philly?"

"Yes . . ."

"Were you honest about what you said about abortion being not heinous. I mean, you're having it, too, you know."

About abortion, I feel we should admit to the slaughter and otherwise be at peace. I told her, "Yes. Sleep well."

I was falling asleep myself when a strange distress signal roused me. A moment of bafflement careened into chaos as I ripped through laundry and Chinese food cartons in search of the fucking beeper. I realized I didn't need it. Phone! Phone the woman who carries your heir! I dialed furiously. The beeping had stopped and I pictured Susan hemorrhaging in bed. On the first ring the receiver picked up.

"Good boy."

I launched into a tirade about girls who cry wolf; secretly I was gratified. Susan needed me. She never could have admitted this, but the beeper spoke it plainly. She needed me more than I needed her. The beeper, I realized, was power.

The next day, though busy, did not include my renting a car. This had some bearing later.

Carrie picked me up at five on the dot. I took the wheel and she the passenger's seat, predictably sullen of course. I'd been uncertain what to wear. I wasn't sure if during the abortion procedure, as in Lamaze, the man was expected to participate. To avoid mussing a good suit I wore sneakers and jeans. Carrie wore black.

She directed me to the crosstown expressway. I asked

where we were going and she named a commuter suburb. "I didn't wanna go someplace local. I don't wanna see someone I know."

Glancing over, I noticed the crucifix she always wore she wasn't wearing today. In respect for her feelings, I turned off the top forty radio station I'd had on to lighten the mood.

We'd been driving ten minutes. Rain started to fall. The beeper started to beep. "What's that?" Carrie said.

"What's what?"

"That." She pointed to my belt.

An instrument from hell, I wanted to say. Instead I lied: "My new broker must want me to phone him. We're very high tech these days."

"Isn't the stock market closed by now?"

"There are other exchanges. Money's global, Carrie." I turned off the beeper and switched the radio back on.

Susan was testing me again. She wasn't due for a month. And if she did think her contractions had begun, chances were they were false or, at worst, very early—with luck, her labor would last fifteen or twenty hours and I'd only miss the beginning. But a month premature? No way. She wasn't a ghetto mother. I turned the beeper back on. It was blessedly silent.

Carrie directed me off the next exit. "How did you hear of this place?" I asked her, calming.

"On the ladies' room wall at the bus station. There was even a map."

"That's not funny, Carrie." She wasn't smiling. "Is this place respectable?"

"The best," she said. "All their hangers are sterilized."

"Now come on!" Then I saw her chin tremble. Her attempt to prepare, to toughen herself, by hating me began to crumble before my eyes. I moved my hand from the stick shift to her leg. "I'll be glad when it's over."

"I'll bet." The beeper beeped, startling both of us. It beeped and kept beeping over the sound of the rain on the car roof. I yanked it off my belt and held it before me like a hand mirror, like a crystal cube in which I could conjure the face of my tormenter. "Must be important," Carrie said dryly.

"It can wait."

"You sure? You can drop me off. I'll find some guy to drive me there—for a blow job, maybe." Clearly she'd recovered some of her toughness. Her hatred of me was galvanized, armored. She'll survive, I thought with relief.

"Don't keep testing me," I said. "I want to be here."

She laughed. "To make sure, I know." Her laugh was cold steel and resolved me in my plan. If the worst had happened, if Susan indeed was having her baby, then I'd ditch Carrie at the clinic and drive her car back to the city, back to Susan. Carrie couldn't hate me more than she did already. Her hatred would protect her. I'd be doing her a favor.

An insane person's plan, it never would have occurred to me if Susan's beeper hadn't been beeping six inches from my face. So I threw the thing out the window. In the sideview mirror I saw it bounce into traffic and die.

We approached a new-looking brick building across from a shopping mall. "Here," Carrie said. Inside, to my chagrin, the receptionist said yes, if we wished, I could accompany Carrie through the procedure, hold her hand or whatever.

Begging off, I said I was squeamish, but that I'd rejoin her in the recovery room. A nurse led her away down a carpeted hallway decorated with plantings and cheery prints. Carrie's eyes gazing back at me were angry and scared. I mouthed to her, *I like you*, impulsively. Her anger and fright turned to amazement, her face taking a stunned, euphoric look, as if she'd been injected with painkiller. It's possible she'd misunderstood me.

I paid the receptionist in advance, with a credit card. Before taking a seat in the lobby to wait for Carrie to come out, I thought to call Susan, in case. On a pay phone I dialed her private number at Neil's, getting an answering machine. "Just me. Checking in. Catch ya later." The receiver was slick with sweat from my hand.

I dialed Gray Realtors. Alison answered. When she heard my voice she hung up. My pulse upshifted.

I dialed once more. Alison answered, heard my voice and hung up. Dialing again, I jabbed the buttons with the blank-minded grit of a bombardier punching a target code on his home town. "Alison!"

"What?"

"Where's Susan?"

"Susan who?"

"Don't start. Is Neil with her?"

"Neil and Dominique went away for the weekend."

"With Susan home alone pregnant?"

"Susan insisted. She said she had you in case of emergency."

"And here I am."

"And there you are."

"Don't hang up! Just tell me, is it happening?"

"Is what happening, Philip?"

"The baby, goddamn it!"

She paused, loving this. I felt movement:

"Don't hang up."

She hung up. But in the affirmative.

Seeing no other course, I gave the receptionist cash for Carrie's cab fare home. The woman was horrified I was leaving, abandoning Carrie here. I didn't have time to explain my side of it, much less to win her support.

Outside it rained from a dusky sky. I could blame the rain, the dim light, my speed or my messing with the tape deck for making me wreck Carrie's car halfway between the clinic and the hospital. The car jumped the shoulder of the expressway off-ramp and plunged down an embankment, planting its snout like a foraging pig into a mud bog at the bottom.

I was unhurt. Too bad. A minor, profusely bleeding head-wound would have come in handy later, for sympathy. I did suffer a bump on the forehead, coming to to a radio traffic report after five or six seconds unconscious. I turned off the ignition, climbed out of the car and out of the mud bog. Perhaps due to the head bump, the world possessed the vibrancy of an hallucination, brain chemicals mixing to weird effect. Cars I couldn't see roared by on the expressway high up the embankment. Headlights were searchbeams above me. The rain was a special wonder. Its sound was multilayered, the whisper of a single plummeting raindrop overdubbed a million times, creating a lushness within which I could hear any sound

I wanted, from bloodhounds baying on my trail to a welcoming heavenly choir. Mostly I heard a voice urging, "Flee, fool! Make a new start!" But I didn't flee, precisely because I didn't want a new start. I was twenty-four, far too set in my ways to change. Had I run away then, clambered up the embankment and hitched a ride west toward the fallen sun, all that I'd accomplished in the past three years, everything good and everything bad, would have been for naught.

I saw the lights of a bar under the expressway underpass. There I phoned for a taxi. I was soaked with rain and drank two martinis to still my shivering. As I sat at the bar I wondered what Carrie was doing at this moment, what Susan was doing. Last night I'd felt like an immortal angel, knowing each woman's certain future; tonight I felt like an angel's opposite. I drank another martini. When the taxi arrived I was mildly drunk, yes—but my actions the rest of the night would have been the same regardless. If anything, the booze resigned me to the virtue of humility.

Yesterday's Lamaze tour had shown me where the maternity ward was in the hospital. The elevator was mirror-lined and gave me the feeling of being caged with a wild twin brother. It was in that mirrored box that I first glimpsed the bald spot on the back of my head, a quarter-sized defoliation in a jungle of thick auburn; it was a bad night all around. I exited the elevator with much of the fight drained out of me. My bald head throbbed. Fluorescent lights beat down malevolently. There must have been people around—patients, doctors, orderlies—but in my memory the ward is deserted except for Lyle, Neil's secretary, who was seated by the nurses' station alertly awaiting me.

He stood, hands loose at his sides as if ready to draw six-guns. His grim look brought me up short. "Susan's dead?"

"She's fine, Philip. Go home." I tried to step by him. He cut off my path. "You had your chance. You didn't come through."

"I had a situation."

"You've been drinking. Susan told me it's a problem."

"The fuck! I don't have to talk to you." Again I sidestepped him. Again he cut me off.

"If we fight, security will throw us both out. Is that how you want it?"

"I want you out of my face. I'm here to see my kid." I heard my own words. "How is my kid? *What* is my kid?"

"Susan said to say nothing. But he's a beautiful baby boy."

"Healthy?"

"But undersize. He's a month premature."

"Tell me about it. Nervy bastard."

"Will you leave now? For Susan's sake? She really doesn't want to see you."

"How is she doing?"

"Exhausted. Healthy. Happy."

I accepted this, to my own amazement. It was beyond me. This place, this buzzing hive with its babies and mommies and daddies, its proto-families nestled in semiprivate rooms, this place wasn't my place. I felt able to turn and walk away; hence the only honest course was to do exactly that. I said to Lyle, "One favor. Don't tell Susan I was drunk. Tell her I was . . ." I laughed. "Tell her it was business."

"I'm sure she'll believe it."

"I should thank you for driving Susan over."

"I just got here. Gershom brought Susan. He was with her through the delivery."

"What!" It's true—I yelled. "Not Gershom, no way!" The ward that had seemed deserted all at once seemed overrun. I saw women in bathrobes. I heard babies crying. Nurses and orderlies chased me like asylum guards as I dashed down the corridor, trying as I ran to read nameplates on the doors to find out which room was Susan's—and Gershom's! "No! No! No!" The martinis had spoken. Lyle tackled me from behind.

I got to my feet with help. The door in front of me opened to reveal Susan in a pink robe and slippers. Her face was swollen and pale. "Where is it?" I demanded. "Where's my son?"

"Sleeping."

"I wanna see him." Did I? I was torn. I was saying the words a spurned father ought to say, in hopes the words would get a reaction, in me.

words a spurned father ought to say, in hopes the words would get a reaction, in me.

"If you don't see him now, it will be easier for you never to see him. And I want you never to see him."

"Hey, I fucked up."

She shook her head wearily. "You didn't fuck up. *I* fucked up. I lost sight of what mattered. But today made it okay. Today made it perfect." She began to cry. "Please let it stay perfect, Philip. It's something you can give."

About ten people were listening in. A nurse said, "You should be in bed, Mrs. Graulig. Your stitches—"

"Mrs. Graulig?" I said. "Is that what's happened here? You and him—"

"We've fallen in love. That's what's happened."

"Because of me?"

"Because of the baby. With the baby. With each other." She covered her eyes wearily. "And sure, because of you." The nurse took her arm. Susan pleaded, "Please try and understand. It was a magical day."

"I understand perfectly. But I wonder if I'd been with you, would you have fallen in love with me?"

"You weren't here. Gershom was."

"Where is he now?"

"Home, getting stuff." Her voice raised. "Don't you dare try anything."

"He won't," Lyle said.

"Like hell," I said. "Gershom? Fuck him. You? Fuck you. But I *will* be part of my son's life! Starting tomorrow, when I'll be here at visiting hours like the proud daddy that I am."

"Please don't." The nurse pulled Susan into the room. "I'm begging you, Philip. Let us live!" The closed door muffled her cries. The anguished emotions I'd evoked in her saddened me. I was barely flattered at all.

Down the corridor, Lyle got in the elevator with me. I asked him why he was following me. "To make sure you leave."

"Since when are you Susan's bodyguard?"

"I'm anything for the people I love."

"Don't put yourself out for my benefit."

He offered to drive me home. I was suspicious—something true about gays is that they think everyone else is gay. I said I'd appreciate the favor so long as he pulled no funny stuff. "Trust me, you're safe," he said. "I prefer a good build."

"Jeez, kick me when I'm down, how about?"

From his laugh, he felt like a friend for a second.

Pulling up outside Chinaland, he asked me what my intentions were regarding the baby. I told him I would fight for custody; but in my mind I was thinking, What baby? In the next interlude I thought Lyle's sexual pass might come. It didn't, of course. Good thing. In my state of mental disrepair, there's no telling what I'd have done, and one thing I didn't need that night was another odd biographical tidbit.

Upstairs, I called Carrie's apartment. I was dead calm as I dialed, prepared for her outrage, her entirely justified invective against me. I wasn't prepared for no answer. The phone rang and rang. My imagination went wild, projecting her death by abortion malfunction, by suicide, projecting me standing at her graveside with the weight of the world on my shoulders. Then I realized where Carrie was. Peace came over me, peace in knowing I was part of a plan that now must run its course. The plan was my own. Its course was down. It had a kind of beauty.

"Yes?" Timmy Donley said when I dialed his number.

"How is she?"

Silence. I thought he might hang up. He launched a speech he doubtless had been rehearsing all night: "What you did to Carrie was the most despicable, sadistic thing I've ever seen. Forget she's my wife. Forget you got her pregnant. Forget you made her get an abortion—but to abandon her in that situation? To steal her car? Philip, it scares me to think what makes you tick."

"Is she okay?"

"They gave her Valium after the procedure. She was whacked out and traumatized—and utterly alone."

"I had a situation."

"Can you imagine her fear? Her humiliation?"

"As long as she's okay now."

"She'll live. That's about all I know."

"Can I talk to her?"

"She's sleeping. Not that it matters."

I nodded as if he could see me. "I'll make good on her car. I wrecked it."

"I'm going to wreck you."

"I figured you might try."

"I can do it. I know all about your scam with Peter Rice."

"You profited also. You'll be indicting yourself."

"I'm sure I'll be fired. So what? I've got evidence on both of you—phone records, notes, receipts. I'm not as stupid as you thought."

"How could you have been?"

"My old school chum," getting wistful now, "nailing my wife for years."

"What's good for the goose is good for the gander." But Timmy wasn't into situational ethics:

"You shithead! You scum!"

I hung up. I'd heard it all before.

Six aspirin made a sour lump in my gut as I tossed in bed. My thoughts flitted over the day's twin imponderables of two babies I'd never seen. I chose to perch on a lesser regret and there settled down to sleep. I regretted that I hadn't apologized to Carrie or Susan. I regretted it—and then again I didn't, for otherwise it was back to those babies. Apologies could wait. The babies were a done deal.

The next morning I was awakened by knocks on my door: the police. They informed me that a complaint of violent harassment had been lodged against me by Mr. and Mrs. Gershom Graulig of—

"I know where they live! Where *she* lives. She has my baby. *Our* baby. Because it was my sperm, officer. It was not Gershom's sperm!"

They told me to stay away or I'd be arrested. They seemed to want to arrest me anyway. I probably should have put clothes on.

The phone rang. It was my attorney, Jeffrey Masters. He

said some cops would soon serve me with a complaint of harassment, but that I shouldn't take it personally. "It's a formality, Philip. Susan and Gershom have every confidence that you won't threaten them again."

"I'll kill them, Jeffrey. Then I'll kill you."

He laughed. "Always a joke, Phil—I love that. But I should tell you I'm recording this conversation." He said that Susan and Gershom intended to adopt the new baby.

"They're kidnappers! I'm the father, I have rights."

"You have abusive tendencies. And I understand there's a drinking problem."

"What!"

"Gershom has testified to an episode, and a Jill MacDougal. Susan tells me you drank heavily at your luncheon dates together. And I gather last night was quite a show."

"Jeffrey, listen—it's precisely because I rarely drink that I appear to be drunk so often. These charges are slander."

"File a counter-complaint."

"Excellent. Do it."

"I'm representing Susan and Gershom. I can't represent you, too. That'd be unethical." He hung up.

I dialed the hospital and asked for Susan's room. The operator said Mrs. Graulig had checked out this morning. "She died?"

"She's been released by special arrangement."

"She had a baby last night! What kind of butcher shop are you running over there?"

"Are you family, sir?"

"I'm the father! The sperm was mine."

She hung up. I dialed Susan at home. No answer. I dialed Carrie's number, then Timmy's. No answer. I'd exhausted my list of friends. Dialing several attorneys listed in the yellow pages, I was told by their services to try Monday morning. The rest of the weekend I watched video porn, ate Chinese food, and drank Wild Turkey from a bottle—I'm a traditionalist in all ways, not least in my vices. Still, I'd never before spent a weekend as carefree, as childlike, not even when I was in college.

"I'm sorry," Peter Rice said. His call woke me at half past eleven, well into what had been a busy Monday morning for Timmy Donley and subsequently for Peter. Timmy had gone to Peter's boss with his allegations of insider trading. Peter's boss summoned Peter in, and together they held a contrite conference call with the bigwigs in Manhattan. Peter sang like a bird of my collusion with him and his mysterious Bluebird Two, the code-named coke dealer who today, I understand, lives in Argentina on the Yankee dollars he washed through the account I managed for Peter. Peter's phone call to me was a courteous apology for pinning the blame on me—for which, I understand further, he later received gentler treatment under the law. I've always considered this unfair. I told officials from the Securities Exchange Commission that I happily would have sung like a bird if only given the chance.

Immediately, I phoned the new brokerage where I'd arranged, after my tiff with Timmy several days ago, to transfer my stock portfolio. I was told the transfer, due today, had been held up unaccountably. My heart sank. Soon I confirmed that my entire account, worth more than a million bucks, had been frozen. I had eighty dollars in the bank; on my bureau, two tens and a five. I called Nick Bakes at Melina's Little Bud Shop:

"The building's for sale, Nick. Because we're friends, I'm giving you first crack."

"I can't afford."

"Three hundred fifty thousand and it's yours."

"Is not possible."

"Don't lie to me! It's obscene the money you're making over there. Three thirty."

"Philly—"

"Three fifteen! Three hundred fifteen thousand. Peanuts."

"You take paper?"

"Cash money."

"You should talk to Frank, maybe," Nick said. "He has the big wallet now."

"He came by the shop Friday?" I asked.

"Him and the Telma woman. And the Cadillac."

"Forgive and forget?"

"I believe yes. He was very okay."

"So buy the building together. Like old times."

"You kidding me? He's a maniac."

"Make me an offer!" I was desperate. Without cash I couldn't get a lawyer, my stocks, or my kid. Nick asked what my rents were upstairs, how much were property taxes. He put the phone to his chest and consulted with his partner. She took over:

"Mr. Halsey? Melina here. How are you? I am fine. We will pay two hundred fifty thousand. Take it or leave it. Thank you."

"I'd be losing money!"

"Twenty percent down right away, for binder. The rest at closing." Fifty grand up front. It seemed like a million to this sudden pauper. I could use the money to retain an attorney *plus* buy the BMW I'd ordered. I told Melina yes. She said have the agreement drawn up, they'd sign it tomorrow—my check would be waiting at the flower shop. The story of America: Wherever they hail from, immigrant women are ruthless with the buck.

I decided to have the Bakeses' lawyer, Bill Kelly, handle the sale, since he knew the property well. He'd just gotten off the phone with Frank when I called him. Kelly told me, "Frank's in deep shit and he says 'cause of you. Something about he can't get his money—his stockbroker says it's all hot. You get tips, do ya, Phil? Pass one my way."

"Frank is crazy."

"Well, sure, but he's some kinda ticked at you."

"How ticked?"

"I cooled him down. We got a meeting tomorrow morning with some brokerage legals. I told Frank let's hear 'em out. Nobody has to die, right? Thing is," he went on, "money's real important to Frank. It's like his whole identity."

Kelly agreed to bring a sales agreement to Melina's Little Bud Shop tomorrow afternoon. I hoped to get details from him at that time about Frank's morning meeting at the brokerage, so I'd know what to expect in my case. I'd steer clear of the brokerage till then, and keep my phone off the hook. With fifty grand in hand by tomorrow, I could hold out for days.

I dialed Carrie's apartment. "You're home," I said breezily. "I'm getting some things. I'm moving back in with Timmy."

"Oh. Is that good?"

"It's real good. He's been great."

"I'm really sorry about Friday."

"I'm not. I have no regrets."

"About your car—"

"The city towed it. When I get an estimate, I'll expect a check from you."

"Sure. Absolutely. So—"

She hung up.

"—have you thought about us?"

I put on a suit and walked to the corner bus stop carrying my empty briefcase. It was midafternoon. I rode the bus until the driver made me get off. I rode another bus. When rush hour came the working people crowded about me as if for warmth. Exhaustion in their faces held a promise of repose. My admiration for these good citizens quickly yielded to envy. I wanted the stability they seemed to possess—the regular hours, a home and family, marigolds in the window box and pet pigeons on the roof. When you idealize what you once dismissed, you know you're losing grip.

I ate a fine dinner at a restaurant I'd frequented during my first months of exile. I'd forgotten the sisterly indulgence with which waitresses wait on polite young men dining alone, forgotten how much I savored it. I got back on the bus and rode for another few hours. Me and the driver and two snoring old drunks. Back at my apartment I fell into bed a free man as usual. It was the last really good time I had for years.

Once cut off from managing my stock portfolio, I lost all

interest in financial news, the market reports and business-page columnists that on usual mornings I memorized. I'd burned out on finance, and secretly welcomed my woes as an opportunity to make a career change wherein my skills with money might give way to skills as a people person. Certainly in the coming weeks I would be dealing with people as never before, dealing with lawyers and SEC agents, not in order to profit but to save myself and my son, goals any good Christian would honor. My boom years were over; it was time to entrench and consolidate. They say having a child rearranges a person's priorities. Federal indictment works also.

In keeping with my new humanism, I skipped the *Times* and the *Wall Street Journal* the next morning and bought a stack of supermarket tabloids. I trace my love of celebrity gossip to that languid morning when over brunch I discovered the range of human experience and foible these tabloids so reassuringly chronicle; indeed, were I not telling this story to you, I would have tried to sell it to them. It was with real contentment that I folded the papers and made my way to Melina's Little Bud Shop. My problems were nothing compared to the two-headed midget or the anorexic movie star—yet we three (or four) shared kinship as the world's favored suffering, those privileged to abide and triumph through gross misfortune. I would triumph. My horoscope said so.

I walked whistling from the bus stop to the flower shop. Inside, the stink of flowers reminded me of a wake, as did the stricken stares of Nick and Melina. At first I thought Nick's mother had died, but she was in position behind the register, albeit with her own stare less stricken than perplexed. The attorney, Bill Kelly, flipped the "Closed" sign outward on the front door. Turning to me, he said Frank Bakes had killed himself. "Blew his brains out. In the Caddie an hour ago."

Melina gave a cry at hearing the news uttered again. I heard old Mrs. Bakes sigh. The vexation on her face bespoke the utter illogic of losing a child. Losing a parent makes sense—we bury our parents and our children bury us, is one definition of a good life. Nick was murmuring in Greek to Melina. She shook her head, her fists pressed to her eyes. He tried to hug her but she drew away. I wanted to tell her that her guilt over Frank's death was needless. Melina had left him more than a year ago, surely a decent interval. He since had found Thelma, found me. "Suicide is nobody's fault," I said.

Bill Kelly gave the suggestion of a smirk. He sidled up to me and whispered, "Frankie got snared in your little racket. They told us at the meeting this morning that at the very least he was gonna lose all his money. His broker, Donley, blames you."

"Frank knew the risks."

"He didn't know shit."

"He'd have to be pretty thick—"

"He *was* thick. That's the point."

"What's your point?"

"Hey, I didn't say nothin' to these folks, if that's your worry. No use to spread the hurt more."

"I appreciate that." In fact, Kelly's secrecy in my behalf made me feel worse, feel responsible. I *was* responsible, but I preferred to keep that between me and my face in the mirror.

"Of course," he said, "your price for this building just went down. You were asking two fifty? You'll take two hundred."

"Why would I do that?"

"If I tell 'em about your thing with Frankie, there'll be no deal at all."

"I'll get another buyer."

"How soon? There's a posse after you."

"You heard that this morning?"

"You're the talk of the brokerage. I believe they mentioned penalties being three times profits." He eyed me. "*Ouch.*"

I was stuck. For $200,000 I'd be selling at a huge loss, but I had no alternative. "Do I still get my binder?"

"Fifty K, up front. Check's all made."

"Can these people get it together to sign? I mean, I don't want to be crass here . . ."

"Ask 'em."

"No," Nick snapped in answer to my question. "The property is bloody today. We will not buy."

"Not for two hundred thousand?"

Melina said, "Not today, and never."

"It's a real bargain," I began, but Mrs. Bakes senior interrupted in Greek aimed at Nick and Melina, then in English aimed at me:

"Yes to buy, Philly! I can cry for Frank next tousand years. We have a deal to make you today." She gestured sharply. "Melina! Nikos! Sign the paper!" The old girl had come through for me. I was touched.

I laid the bank check in my bricfcase—I'd get the balance when they secured a mortgage. I shook hands with Nick and Melina, giving them my condolences. I bowed in gratitude to Mrs. Bakes. The lawyer walked me to the door. "You were a real angel today," I complimented him.

"Wait'll you see my bill."

"Good luck. I expect to declare bankruptcy by then," which took the grin off his face. "Just kidding," I said, hopefully.

Rich again, I treated myself to a taxi and went to my bank to deposit the money. At the window, my teller mentioned that a man was here asking about my account. I ducked instinctively. An investigator-type was perusing a computer printout on the branch manager's desk. I snuck out fast with my check in my fist. To deposit it would have been to donate it to the United States Treasury, going against everything I believe in.

I know when to surrender, and I know *how* to surrender. The biblical precedent supported my inclination to face my father as a penniless prodigal rather than as one who cravenly clings to his last few thousand dollars. Money in itself means little to me—it's to buy things with, nothing more. I determined to unload all my assets ere I returned to the cradle of Stalls Associates. I considered burning the check. I considered blowing it at the race track. Ultimately, I endorsed it over to the United Jewish Appeal, New York City, and mailed it from the Providence train station. The gesture struck me as witty and ironic. Even so, I don't regret it.

On the train ride to Boston, I fell asleep with my duffel bag and briefcase on the overhead rack. I woke to find both had been stolen. I had to laugh. Even as a nonbeliever I knew the Lord was testing me.

I'd never been entirely out of touch with Stalls Associates.

Over the years I'd received office financial statements and the minutes of quarterly trustee meetings. Recently I'd been notified of the next meeting—scheduled for tomorrow, as it happened. Though it would be cowardly to appear there unannounced (leaping into the breach to meet a quick bullet), I hoped it might smack of the cool audacity bureaucrats tend to respect.

I got a hotel room on a credit card near the offices of Stalls Associates. I couldn't sleep. I thought about my child somewhere—I didn't know his name. I thought about my father—his name I knew too well. I thought about Frank Bakes. How strange it was to have caused his death when I could barely recall what he looked like.

Frank blew his brains out in the Cadillac bought with money I'd made him. I tried to imagine the exact effect of his act on the car's upholstery and brightwork. Did he shoot up or sideways? Lead or hollow point? I was missing the art of it. Frank's suicide wasn't a random impulse. Rather, he pointedly blew his brains out in the car of his dreams, wit and irony splattered everywhere. If a man like Frank Bakes could turn his death into a philosophical statement, then perhaps there was hope for me. A person's lowest moment can be the valley from which he postulates a cloud-obscured pinnacle in the sky, his worst offenses merely the balance to the best he can be, or could have been. The laws of physics, finance, and human endeavor require, I think, such a consistent balance of deed and consequence. Frank gave his life to affirm those laws; gave his life, in a way, for me. I would thank him if I could.

My father's secretary, Doris Zuppa, intercepted me outside Stalls Associates' conference room the next morning, but I forced my way past her. Father, looking up, bid me take a seat at the table, then continued the meeting as if he'd been expecting me.

My mother had visited me several times during my exile,

occasions never pleasant. It had been all I could do not to scream that her husband was a phony, their marriage a loveless farce. I'd kept silent mainly out of vanity; withholding from her the secret of Father's Jewish past made his hypocrisy seem more contemptible to me, my banishment more heroic. If my relations with Mother had held steady through four years of minimal life support, my relations with Father survived a deeper dormancy. That is, within minutes of our reunion in 1984 they bloomed again into the mutant flower of old.

I slouched at the opposite end of the conference table as he droned to the trustees of economic forecasts and investment strategies. Distaste informed his every glance at me. Yet I felt at ease, sitting there. I knew he'd make me squirm before I got one dime of assistance, one gratis attorney to finesse me through my difficulties. Yet I had no doubt that after some rote exchange of contrition and censure, he'd help me. As my trustee, he had a fiduciary duty to save my ass. I could sue him if he refused. It pays to know your rights.

The meeting ended. The trustees, all relatives of mine, filed past me with perfunctory greetings. Father asked Stalls Rayburn, my mother's uncle and the office's sage-in-residence, to remain behind. The two men sat side by side at the end of the table. Panic suddenly seized me: in that instant I recalled the release I'd signed four years ago, absolving Stalls Associates of all liability in my future affairs. Any aid I received must come from charity and parental kindness. I regretted the birthdays I'd forgotten, the Father's Days and high holidays. Thinking fast, I bent down to hitch up my socks, giving him a good look at my beginning bald spot. I wanted to show what stress I'd been under and to bond with him, a fellow baldy, as one similarly cursed.

The first words in four years he said to me were, "What do you need, Philip?"

"What do I need?" Repeating your interrogator's question gives you time to think. "What do I need?"

"I assume you're here for a reason."

"A reason?"

He looked terrible, was what threw me. More precisely, he

looked too good. His complexion had an artificial, orangey hue, as if toasted under a sun lamp. He'd lost weight. The skin on his face seemed shrink-wrapped around his skull. The effect wasn't so much cadaverous as it was simply not him. Never could the David Halsey I had known wear a tapered double-breasted suit. Never could he have exchanged his L. L. Bean walking shoes for a pair of tasseled loafers, nor faked a suntan or sported a pink necktie. Something severe had befallen him. At once I assumed he'd lost his mind or taken a mistress. If the former, he'd be putty in my hands. If the latter, I thought, he'll be anxious to atone for his secret transgression; giving succor to the son he detested was one way to do just that. My confidence gained. When he repeated his question, I shot back an answer meant to provoke him, to flush from behind its garish facade the truth of his transformation:

"What do I need? Lawyers, guns, and money. *Hah!*" I gave a loony grin. Deal with that, you crazy fuck!

Father said nothing. Stalls Rayburn cleared his throat. Pushing eighty and a full head of hair—I hated him. "Is that supposed to be funny, Philip?"

"Not at all, Cousin Stalls. It's my opening bargaining position. From which, if you play your cards right, I can be jewed down to where I'll settle for money and lawyers and forgo weapons altogether. *Hah!*"

He glanced at my father. "I see."

"As to numbers," I went on, "I should think half a mil, two attorneys and two paralegals on twenty-four-hour retainer oughta get me through the weekend. That, and any spare change you might have. *Hah!*" Father's complexion had gone from orange to scarlet. My heart thundered. My mouth kept moving: "Can we order up lunch, fellas? I haven't eaten since yesterday. Chinese is fine by me, or maybe bagels and lox—"

"Please stop."

"You said something, Dad?"

A pause. "You've changed, Philip."

"Losing my hair, I know."

"I don't mean superficially. You seem afraid. I didn't think it possible." The bastard was sharp as ever, not insane at all.

"So! Messing around on Mom, eh?"

"What the—" Stalls Rayburn said.

"You're talking gibberish, son. Do you realize that?"

"I am not your son!"

"But you are," he sighed, as if in apology. "Just as I'm your father."

The windowless room felt like a capsule spinning through space. I began to feel sick. To steady myself I fixed my eyes on the knot of Father's necktie, a pink triangle that my fevered mind vaguely remembered as representing some small category of age-old persecution. I'm ignorant of history. Oh, had a yellow star been dangling at Father's throat, or a crucifix or a human bone fragment, some blatant, implacable, bloodsoaked signifier, I might have been shamed into respectful composure. As it was, I focused on his pink necktie as a clothing accessory of such poor taste it was the easiest thing to mock:

"What's with the California look, Dad? No more Mr. Mensch? You a Baptist now, or what?"

I rocked furiously in my chair. The two men at the end of the table, Stalls Rayburn and my father, began to dissolve. It seemed funny: two men whose blood comprised my own dissolving and bleeding together like watercolors rained on, like A-bomb victims vaporizing. I started laughing. I laughed and coughed and then vomited two cups of morning coffee on the glass-topped conference table. My eyes were swimming as Cousin Stalls rose and approached me. He pressed a handkerchief into my hand. Father didn't move. He stared at me, his complexion again the orange parody of good health. My breakdown had somehow uplifted him. What I said next uplifted him further:

"Daddy, I fucked up. I'm just really sorry."

"We all do, son. We all do."

A thick warmth flared inside my chest. With visible effort Father stood and came to me. He put his hands on my shoulders. I was sobbing out of control. I couldn't stop sobbing. For myself, you see? Because he and I were equals after all.

His secretary sponged up the vomited coffee; I was too sapped to feel humiliated. Two junior attorneys were summoned from a downstairs office. Stalls Rayburn passed out cigars as I detailed, like a returned adventurer, my financial rise and fall. Father was impressed with the stocks and options I'd picked legitimately over the years; he offered frowns but otherwise nonjudgmental reactions to Peter Rice's and my insider trading scheme. So indulgent was the atmosphere, I took more credit than I merited for the scheme's conception and devising, not wanting to seem an utter dupe. I left out the bright side, the sex and prurience that redeemed my exile from being a total waste. And I left out Frank Bakes's suicide and the birth of my child, things too sacred to tell; left out as well the bit about the abortion.

I talked a good two hours. Consensus built among my listeners to surrender on all counts, to settle my case with minimum fuss. I felt disappointed, fooled again, enticed into capitulation when I still had straws to cling to. The upshot was I never did jail time. Over the following months, Stalls family lawyers, citing my youth as a mitigating factor, slaked the SEC with payoffs totalling half a million dollars in fines on top of all profits returned. I was wiped out. This hurt. Being banned from trading securities for a period of three years hurt, too, though it was a relief at first. Eventually I began trading through an account in my mother's name—it's my craft, after all, the one thing I'm good at, the one way I contribute.

The lawyers departed to go make the phone calls that would start my guilty pleas rolling. Father and Cousin Stalls mused aloud what should be done with me, a college dropout and admitted felon. As their job suggestions narrowed to clerical versus janitorial, I felt compelled to speak:

"The fact of the matter is, I'm gifted at money management. Just extend me a moderate, interest-free loan, and I'll be on my way—much chastened, a good boy ever more."

Father chuckled. "I think the feds would complain."

"Why me? Corporations steal billions. I'm a punk!"

"True enough. But while I can forgive your indiscretions, I

will not dodge the law. Until your case is settled and your debts paid, you'll be needing gainful employment."

Cousin Stalls proposed a job as "family liaison." Stalls Associates, he said, had grown remote from younger family members and as a result had become, in their eyes, a coterie of gray old men who toiled in secrecy over their money like witches over a cauldron. Compounding the problem was today's fashion, unlike the 1960s when wealth was taboo, to live like kings as soon as they inherited their trusts. "They don't understand our defensive investment posture," Stalls said. "They think we're old farts who are either incompetent or hiding something—just as you thought four years ago."

"But now I know better."

The old fart smiled. "Indeed. There can be no finer ally than one who has seen the other side."

Father chipped in, "Your example made quite a sensation in the family. You were rumored to be an international financier."

"And now that the ugly truth is known?"

"Many will still respect you. Flamboyant success and failure is very attractive to some people."

"As opposed to failing in private, yes? Which is so common, after all." My comment jacked up the tension between us. Cousin Stalls went on obliviously, "You'd be invaluable to us, Philip. You, better than anyone I can think of, can instruct the next generation that wealth is a responsibility. They'll believe you."

"He's not an outsider," Father said. "We prefer that."

"He's blood," Stalls agreed. "Blood matters."

"Even if it's polluted?" I asked blithely.

Stalls cupped his ear. "Say again?"

"I said: Even if it's polluted?"

Father explained, "Philip is referring to his, to *my*, Jewish heritage. He thinks he's shocking you."

I stared at him. Things had changed around here, evidently. "He knows?"

"It's an old story. We really don't think about it."

Was I surprised? After a second, no. He'd always kept one

step ahead of me. But I resented his attitude, his dismissal of a secret that had held such power in my mind. I resented it on my account but more so on his, that he should dare downplay what undeniably had been a crucial crossroads in his life. As I considered, however, I sensed something more. Father's new look, his embrace of me, his offhandedness about a past he once had guarded so ominously—the contradictions were too many to believe, an alibi too pat. There's desperation here, I thought. Father hasn't changed at all. He's merely *trying* to change. I asked my cousin, "When did you find out? That David Halsey was David Holscheimer?"

Stalls turned to my father, "When did we have that talk?"

"Four years ago, perhaps?" I said.

"No. More recently," Stalls said. "Last year. When your dad got sick."

"Sick, you say?"

"Well sure. The cancer."

I looked at Father. "The cancer?"

He'd been watching our exchange impassively, as one might watch an ax being sharpened, unsure whom it's meant for. "Philip doesn't know I was ill," he said to Stalls.

"Oh. Gee. But it's fine now, right, David? Remission and whatnot?"

"So they tell me."

There was an awkward pause. Stalls creakily rose from his chair. "I think I'll let you two catch up. But think about that job, Philip—"

"I accept."

"—because we need you. And I daresay," he slapped my back jovially as he passed behind me, "you need us."

Alone now, Father and I sat in silence. I saw the picture complete. My return—my return, that is, in ruins—had imparted a last imprimatur to the codified, cautious, Brahmin existence he'd chosen as a young man. My own existence beyond his controlling benefaction must have been irritating to him. Now he could sleep well. "Everyone knows," I asked, "about your deep dark past?"

"Everyone. To have kept it a secret seems silly now."

"Its importance was only in your mind."

"Yes. Exactly."

"And it's not important any longer."

"I simply don't think about it. I used to, of course."

"*I* think about it. I don't know *what* I think about it, but I do." I laughed. "So you're a Gentile now?" Our balance of power had shifted. I'd hit bottom and bounced. I was guessing he lacked the same resilience.

"A Christian," he said. "Congregational. I was baptized last year, while I was in the hospital."

"A deathbed conversion? How quaint."

His face darkened. "Perhaps you will face death better."

"Oh, I'm sure I'll do it just like you."

We had a moment of mutual staring. His expression was sadly expectant, as if he knew I was keeping secrets. Strolling around the table, I withdrew from my coat pocket and laid before him the old passport photograph of Philip Holscheimer, Father's father, my grandfather, baldheaded and glaring up from the table like an angry insomniac. "Found this the other day," I said, repeating Father's words to me about the photo, spoken when he'd given it to me four years ago. On a last-minute impulse I'd brought it along today as a protective talisman. Father's glance flicked down nervously.

"That man is dead to me. We killed each other."

"I doubt it was that dramatic."

"Do you? On what basis."

"On the basis of my own similar experience. Which came thanks to you."

"So I'm to blame," he gestured toward me, "*for this*?"

"I was your experiment. Through me, you replayed your own family disaster. I fizzled—the experiment succeeded."

"You give me too much credit."

I tapped the photo with my fingertip. "Why else inflict this bombshell on me just as I was making my getaway."

"Because it represented the truth—about me, about you."

"Hogwash."

"All right," he said slowly. "Tell me."

"You wanted to fuck me up."

"Oh, for God's sake, Philip—"

"You wanted to mentally sabotage me like your father did to you. It was strictly payback."

"*No!*" His orange face went red. "I gave you that photograph as a warning. I wanted to show you there's nothing new under the sun—it's all been done before, and badly. It was a warning, and a plea."

"A plea for what?"

He hesitated. "Not to leave."

"Your precious Stalls Associates?"

"It's more than that to me. It represents a choice I made. It's who I am."

"Pathetic."

Slowly, "That's not for you to say."

"Why? I apply the term to myself as well. I've come back to you as nothing, with a past I want to bury. Sound familiar?"

"Philip—"

"You needed me to fail! And I provided." I was standing next to him. A vein throbbed in the parchment skin of his temple. I knew something about the blood in that vein, its addiction to regret.

Remarkably, he smiled. "No, Philip. I wanted you to thrive. I tried to help. I purposely mailed you our quarterly reports and the minutes of our trustee meetings so you'd know what we were up to, what companies we liked. It wasn't much, I know. But it was something I could do."

"They were useful," I admitted, surprised.

"I'm glad."

"But what about this photograph? And the legal steps you took to block my freedom, and the money you took in penalties? You tried to wreck me from the start."

"I was angry—and jealous. But I came to really hope you would find the success you craved, in all aspects of your life, even as the Philip Holscheimer who scorned his dad to strike out on a path of his own. Especially as that."

My mouth had gone dry. "Well, I'm back."

His eyes had focused somewhere in the air. "But I had it wrong, too. Because I find now that I dearly want you home. I

don't care what you've done. I understand what you've done."
His hesitation seemed to come of exhaustion, of effort.
"Apparently," he said, "I love you."

The moment might have been scripted, so perfectly did I
feel empathy with him, his emotions and mine entwining to the
snapping point. My next line would be one of two, the kind
thing or the truth. "I love you, too," I might have said. From
there I could have improvised, no solid ground under me ever
again, nor under Father either, each of us floating on senti-
ments lovely to say but not durable, not meant to last, like the
pretty webs spiders build time and again, when, in the process
of snaring sustenance, the strands repeatedly break. I told him
the truth instead:

"I fathered a child."

His head cocked toward me slightly. The focus of his eyes
retracted.

"Born last Friday. A son."

I flinched when Father's hand seized my arm like a claw.
He hauled himself to his feet, knocking over his chair behind
him. His arm came around in what I thought would be a punch
in my nose but proved a desperate embrace. "That's wonder-
ful," he rasped at my ear.

"Whaddaya mean?" I pulled away in panic.

"You're a father! You have a son!"

"Well, yeah. But its mom and I aren't married."

"Do you think I care? I want to meet her. I want to meet
him." His eyes were wet. "My son has a son."

"Jesus, Dad. This is out of left field."

"What, that I'm thrilled to be a grandfather?" His grin was
massive. He hugged me again.

"Dad! It's just a baby. And a bastard besides."

He recoiled. "What kind of scummy talk is that?" In a fury
he shook me by the shoulders. "Wake up! Open your eyes and
see!"

"See what?"

"I'm dying, goddamn you! Look at me!"

"I did, you look sharp. I figured aerobics, a tanning
salon—"

Shoving me away, he clawed his face. "The nurse put

makeup on me so I wouldn't look like a corpse. Some fool tailor made me this suit because mine all fall off me. I've lost fifty pounds!"

"And the tie and shoes?" My question brought a stare.

"*Clothes* he notices. Yes," he said, "they're your mother's selection. Bought special for today. She wanted me look *snappy*."

"For the trustee meeting."

"I've been out two weeks. People think I've been on vacation. But I've been taking treatment in the hospital. I've had a relapse." He shook his head. "It's finished, you see?" I studied him afresh; he looked pretty damn bad, it was true. "But a lot of people depend on me around here, so I tried to put on a healthy appearance."

"Why bother?"

"You retain your gift for tact, I see."

"What I mean is, you don't owe anyone anything."

"I owe myself. I've dedicated my life to this family."

"There *is* no family anymore. The connections are monetary, like stock we can't sell."

"Stalls Associates is important to me. It gave me pride and purpose when I thought I would never have either. Because you're right: I came here in 1952 as nothing. I'd quit my homeland, quit my family—"

"Your religion. Your name."

"—which in themselves meant nothing to me, though they symbolized everything. But the cost, I believe, was a certain humanity in myself, a sense of need. My illness last year forced me to confront these things. I found that faith helped—Christian faith, it so happened." He faltered, the words suddenly coming hard; they were too candid maybe, or too prosaic, to be easily uttered outside a church or a TV evangelical show, a foxhole or a hospice. "I've felt less lost since embracing Jesus."

For a moment I couldn't respond. I was both moved and repelled by Father's confession, so stunningly out of character for the man I'd known four years ago. I changed the subject like a coward: "No one told me you were sick. No one contacted me."

"It was my fight. But looking back, perhaps I should have summoned you home. Would you have come?"

"Probably not."

"Only as a last resort."

"So it seems."

"Then I'm grateful for your troubles. And to my soul, I'm grateful for your child, my grandson." His eyes tearing again, he wiped them and smiled fiercely. "It's a good sign, don't you think? After everything we've suffered?"

It had come to me, as he spoke, what I had to do. I didn't want to do it, yet my reluctance was itself compelling; it should never be easy to hurt someone. Our lives, Father's and mine, had momentarily untangled in my mind, and lay now side by side like string, his mangled youth a version of my own, his later life my future. I was angered and awed to find myself, without asking, in possession of the power to make him confront the same vision, its logic of destined beginnings and ends. I couldn't help but wield that power. It seemed a heavenly gift, the kind with two edges.

"About the baby," I said, swallowing, knowing I was pulling a trigger. "I've already given it up for adoption."

His smile hung on. "That can't be true."

"It's true. I've never seen him. I don't even know his name. He's someone else's son now."

I expected fury. Instead, he slumped against the table as if socked in the stomach. He barely kept his feet. He pulled himself hand over hand along the table's edge like a man at the rail of a tossing ship. When he came to the next chair, he collapsed in it. Without looking at me, he asked if the adoption could be voided.

"It's signed and delivered. I wouldn't want to anyway."

"Your child. Your flesh and blood."

"And yours."

"Is it revenge against me? Is that what it is? My God, Philip, I've admitted I was wrong."

"It's for the baby's sake. I'm not fit to be its father. We aren't fit to be its family."

"But to cast him aside!"

"He's with his mother and her family, who love him. They're quality. Well-to-do. And Jewish."

"Am I supposed to see irony in that?"

"I do."

"You are a chilly bastard."

"Maybe it's genetic."

"No!" He slapped the table. "It can't be true." He raised his hand and pointed between my eyes. "You'll regret it. You will die regretting it."

"I believe you."

The bridge between us burned. Father now possessed the supreme revelation men deserve at the end of their lives—the last piece of the puzzle, the nail in the coffin. I'd broken his heart after my breakdown had started to heal it. I truly believed he didn't want it healed. I believed this because I thought I understood him, because I thought we were alike.

There was a very long silence. Sounds of office activity filtered through the closed door. The spinning space capsule of our tortured privacy landed and went still. Father wiped his eyes a last time, his voice as brittle as glass: "You will tell no one. You have no son. You never had a son. Your life before today is a legal issue, and once that's settled, a dead issue."

"That's your style. Not mine."

"Please. Have pity. You'll be free of me soon enough."

"I am sorry."

He stared at me—aghast, amazed—then spit out a laugh that froze my bones. "I believe you think you are. *Now*," he continued with a punctuating grunt, "you'll start at $15,000 a year. For your office, there's a storeroom we can convert . . ."

My head spun at the change of subject. Soon I matched his officiousness and proceeded with him, in the manner of gentlemen, to strangle all but the thinnest stream of communication between us. We'd shared deep truths of ourselves, the deepest being that we would share nothing in the future; the result was honest and rare, if bizarre. We sat at the table and plotted the rest of my professional life. Had we embraced and wept together we could not have been closer in spirit.

Of course, I hadn't surrendered my son. Yet conceiving the lie had seemed inspired and fulfilling it imperative; a price was due in order to rectify Father's retreat from the truth of himself. For the sake of honor, I told myself. His, not mine. My honor doesn't concern me. It's a dead man's consolation.

I phoned my ex-lawyer Jeffrey Masters and told him I would yield to Susan all rights to our child. "Gershom, too?" he asked. "They're back together."

"Sure," I said without hesitation.

Jeffrey explained that adoption takes time. My letter of renunciation of parental rights would begin the process. I told him to write it, I'd sign when I returned to vacate my apartment. My resolve never wavered. Susan's insistence that I never see the baby had been wise. Women's instincts are a marvel when it comes to cutting ties.

A week later I made the trip to Providence. I met Nick and Melina Bakes to complete the sale of my building. They'd buried Frank not long before. Our closing was civil and cold. The money they paid me went straight to the government. From there I went to Jeffrey's to sign the renunciation papers. Waiting with him in his office was Gershom Graulig. He wore his yarmulke, work boots, and overalls, ever the Diaspora peasant. "I thought we should meet," he said stiffly.

A typewritten document lay in triplicate on Jeffrey's desk. Beside the papers was an uncapped pen. Without a word I signed.

"I want you to know," Gershom said, "that your—that the baby—will have a good life."

"That's a big promise."

"He'll have every benefit, is what I mean."

"So did I." This came out more seriously than I'd intended it. I asked him, "What's he look like, anyhow?"

Gershom glanced at the lawyer.

"Relax," I said. "The paper's signed. I'm not gonna renege."

"At birth he looked like Menachem Begin. But already he's favoring Susan."

"And his name?"

Jeffrey cut in: "I think personal questions are a bad idea."

"His name is Sholem," Gershom said. "His middle name is Philip. He can go with either, later. As he wishes."

I stammered, "I'm surprised you'd pick Philip. I don't know why you would have."

"It was Susan's father's name."

"Now I know."

"It's also the baby's father's name."

My chest hurt. The room began the spinning-capsule thing. I could stop it only one way. "The baby's father's name is Gershom."

He stepped toward me, his voice quavering as he began his speech. "About before, when we first met that time? I'm sorry."

"Ah. The ol' spit-in-the-eye routine."

"It was the worst thing I ever did. I apologize sincerely."

I shook his extended hand. Then I got out of there fast.

Several years later I tried, through Jeffrey, to set up a trust fund for Sholem. Susan and Gershom answered thanks but no thanks, I'm sure suspecting an attempt to worm in. But by then I'd accepted the loss of my son, was even rather proud of having given him up. I'd done the right thing for the wrong reasons. There are worse epitaphs.

My father went into a coma four months later. Gone for all intents and purposes, he lay quiet for weeks, barely breathing. Then in a macabre revival, he flailed his arms, kicked off the sheets, and gave occasional bone-chilling moans during his last few days alive. Mother and I took turns at his bedside. Father's secretary, Doris Zuppa, who probably knew him as well as anyone did, sometimes relieved us for a spell. He died on Doris's shift on a Tuesday afternoon.

The SEC hadn't yet formally barred me from trading, so I was at Stalls Associates watching my stock in Alpha Partners plummet. (Tipped onto Alpha by Father's oncologist, I'd bought the stock with money borrowed from Mother.) The company's bankruptcy announcement and Doris's phone call came minutes apart. "We're done," was how she broke the news to me. Her words seemed rather too casual, as if seeing a man die wasn't new to her. It opened my eyes to the possibility that beneath this woman's efficient reserve might lie a whole bunch of secrets.

Doris had begun working at Stalls Associates when I was thirteen and she was just out of secretarial school. She'd immediately got on my bad side by noting to Father my "kind of cute" habit of sending fan letters to TV meteorologists. Nor had she endeared herself to me during my wrangles with Stalls Associates in 1980, rebuffing my phone calls, deflecting my fury with insubordinate blather like "Philip, might it be just a phase?" Doris was a master of gracious expedience in cleaning Stalls messes wherever they happened, discreetly posting bail for relatives jailed for drunk driving, wiring money to casinos all over the world to cover someone's gambling debts. Naturally, I'd wondered if Father was sleeping with her; during puberty I thought everyone was sleeping with everyone else, except me. But Doris and Father together? Unlikely, not least because it seemed to be something that would have done each of them good.

One of Doris's specialities was planning funerals. Father's was a substantial affair. Per his request, the readings were from the New Testament. Two eulogies were given. Stalls Rayburn spoke of Father's love of his adoptive family and nation. The minister who'd baptized him in the hospital last year extolled Father's love of Jesus.

There were men among the pallbearers whose names you'd recognize. Father's ashes were placed in the Stalls family plot, an impressive parcel of monuments and greenery edged with a low granite wall. A stone obelisk dedicated to the patriarch, Samuel Stalls, stands in the center of the plot. "We're the best," is a popular toast at family gatherings. My younger cousins say it jokingly, thinking the idea passé and elitist. But they, like me, no doubt will clamor to be buried within this fancy enclosure when the time comes, for if it affords little else these days, our birthright entitles us not to lie in potter's fields or anonymous pits, small comfort till you lose it. Reminding my cousins of exactly this fact would be part of my job as family liaison in the coming years. I would counsel conservatism, a defensive posture. I would preach the granite wall.

Looking back now, I believe I performed those duties with diligence but also with sensitivity. I know that youth must have its head at least to the precipice. I sought compromise with those cousins who itched for control of their money. I offered to work with them in their heartfelt projects—the movie they wanted to finance, the homeless shelter, the dreamhouse, the get-richer-quick scheme, the eradication of world hunger—gently steering them toward the awareness that such dreams are pitfalls, traps set by people with less.

As family liaison I was confessor to my young cousins, marriage and drug counselor, friend and bitter enemy. I put private investigators on their prospective spouses and business associates, even on my cousins themselves whom I suspected of gross immaturity. Ego was not involved. I was gratified to enlighten them about the duplicitous ways of the world; beyond that I took no pleasure. Indeed, I was left quite cold by it all, by the constant upwelling of hope and naiveté that I was obligated to squash. I often felt bored and depressed. Still, I strove to maintain the polished demeanor people had come to expect of me—come to expect especially since my father's funeral, when I buried the esteemed gentleman in the afternoon and hosted a thousand mourners at a catered reception that evening. A standard was set that day, a sort of scepter passed.

At the reception many visitors complimented my staunch bearing. In truth I'd been inspired to it earlier that day. Mother and I had been standing at graveside, listening to the minister drone assuringly beneath a whispery rainfall. She held the urn containing Father's ashes in two gloved hands. When she knelt to deposit the urn in the ground, I mumbled, to myself I thought, "Someone ought to say Kaddish." At my ear, very softly, came this:
"Kaddish."

I turned to discover Doris Zuppa standing close behind me, stretching to keep a black umbrella over my mother. "I meant the prayer," I said, taken aback by her intrusion.

"Do you know the words?" she asked me, the inappropriately blithe tone of her voice an intimate, even naughty underlayer to the minister's harrowing "dust to dust" speech, like silk sheets beneath a shroud.

"Not a chance."

"Let's see . . ." She raised her chin as if preparing to recite for the classroom. "'Hallowed be His great name, in the world He has created . . .' That's how it starts, I think." Her voice was hushed, confiding. "'May there be abundant peace from heaven, and life for us and for all Israel. Let us say, Amen.' That's the refrain," she explained. "'Let us say, Amen.'"

"'Let us say, Amen,'" I repeated, fascinated. At which Mother, straightening beside me, brushing crumbs of dirt from her glove tips, joined in with a brave smile:

"Amen."

So Kaddish, or at least a fragment of the Jewish memorial prayer, was spoken at Father's interment courtesy of his loyal secretary, who, it turned out, had learned it during the many funerals she'd attended recently. In the few months since I'd returned home, I'd encountered Doris only at the office. Our graveside exchange, aptly blending reverence and irreverence, marked our first natural contact.

Mother wept hard as she and I climbed into the limousine together. "He was a good man," she said. "He tried to be good."

"You loved him. He loved you." My rote condolences shamed me.

"Did you love him?"

"Aw, Mother, you know the answer to that." I felt trembly, as if about to cry over the fact that I couldn't cry. A son ought to love his father—be a sap for him first and admirable second, to paraphrase Carrie Donley. Through the car window I observed black-clad relatives climb into their automobiles. I resented the unqualified sorrow in their faces. It made me think there was something wrong with me.

I saw Doris Zuppa heading to her car. At once I conjured a

phantasmagoric impression of a woman half Susan, half Carrie, overlaying it like a double exposure on the image of Doris as she trotted quickly through the rain. A man came into the picture behind her, bearded, frail, laboring to keep up with her. The impression made a dazzling fit with my memory of those women as I guessed he was Doris's husband. After that, it was easy to be gracious for my relatives at the funeral reception. I marveled at Doris's deft performance as both employee and de facto hostess, Mother being medicated past any good use. Doris and I mingled singly among the guests while connecting by eye contact or familiar smiles whenever our paths crossed. She was thirty-three at the time, and in her dress of mourning looked a luminous forty. Her hair is black and her eyes are gray. Her manner is of a stylish gym teacher; to my mind it's a casing, like a bullet's brass, in which Doris barely contains potential she's not proud of. From that day through my subsequent tenure as Stalls Associates' family liaison, she was my beacon in a sea of blood relations. She was married, of course, so it was strictly hands off. You thought I was slipping, I know.

My first three years at Stalls Assciates saw the stock market boom incredibly. The Dow-Jones Industrials broke two thousand. The financial pages brimmed with success stories and profiles of glamorous capitalists. The media backlash against them would soon come, a gleeful yuppie-bashing occasioned by a really very few bad apples. Trend and countertrend are such quicksand. I was glad to be out of fashion.

I cut a strange and forbidding figure in those days— priestly, rather, with slicked-back hair and an unchanging daily uniform of a white shirt, silver necktie, and black suit. Between 1984 and 1987 I didn't have sex, keeping chaste mainly out of idealization of Doris. I was saving myself for her—in vain, I knew. Bothered by guilt, as vague and persistent as a fingertip papercut, I needed to perform a correspondingly vague and persistent penance. Deluded rapture would serve.

My cousins pestered me with introductions to their daughters and nieces to a point where I got annoyed. When Stalls Rayburn tried to fix me up with his grandniece, I impulsively blurted that I was homosexual. "Oh?" he gulped. "My mistake." He gave me no trouble, so the old guy deserves credit. Homosexual to him was an unspeakable word, like menstruation and Roosevelt.

By then I was running Stalls Associates as much by default as by ambition. During my SEC probation I never traded a dime in my own name, though I was controlling the investment of millions of dollars by 1987, when I turned twenty-seven. In the dearth of business-minded family members, older trustees had stayed past their effectiveness. They were pleased to pass their duties to me and remain on ceremoniously. I dominated investment meetings to everyone's profit, my voice ever for caution, even during the market boom. I wasn't happy, however. Living like a monk is fine if you're rewarded with heaven; it gets old if that's all there is. And the prospect of Mother as my life mate seemed a lonesome road indeed. You can imagine my feelings on hearing that Doris's husband was terminally ill.

I didn't know the man. I presumed that Doris's existence outside the office was as meaningless as my own. I presumed her marriage, her past, her whole private life, were intervals of dormancy between moments spent near me. She worked only part time during the last months of her husband's illness. I looked forward to her return to the office—meaning, frankly, that I looked forward to his death. I intended to ask her to be my personal secretary. But Doris gave notice two weeks after she buried him. She would stay on to train her replacement, then leave my life forever. I was stunned. I'd sent expensive flowers to the funeral home and arranged a hefty donation from Stalls Associates to the charity named in her husband's obituary. I'd be lying if I didn't say I'd considered them investments.

In the days before she was scheduled to quit, I totally lost focus on work. I resisted urges to follow her home after work, peeling off her trail only at the subway entrance. Often I then wandered to the Common to feed the ducks and swans on the water, a contemplative habit I'd adopted in recent years. Others share it. During work hours on business days, many young professionals come down from their offices to the pond and plain of the Common like cave dwellers down from surrounding mountains. A few smoke dope or meet somebody's spouse. Most, like me, feed the filthy waterfowl and in the process are refreshed. A number of us go there regularly. Like patrons of a porno theater, we're humbled by our waywardness and rarely speak to one another, rarely make eye contact. Our moments on the Common aren't moments of real life. Real life is lived in the mountains, in the caves we're bound to return to.

One afternoon, after lying in ambush for her in the elevator, I asked Doris what she'd be doing in the future. "I'll be managing an AIDS hospice in Newton. The money's not much, but that's not the point."

"An AIDS hospice? Wow," I chirped as if she'd said she would be starring in a Hollywood movie. "Stalls Associates is always looking for worthy charities—"

"For tax purposes, I know. In fact, I want to thank you for arranging that donation from Stalls Associates after my husband died. It was very generous."

"Oh, was what where it went? I just told the accountants to send the money where the obit specified."

"That's how it works, I know. I made similar payments for your father all the time. But it's appreciated just the same."

I kept on breezily, "I had no idea that hospices were an interest of yours."

"It's not like I seek out fellow hobbyists. People can be snide about do-gooders. And because it's AIDS they get scared. You particularly, I thought."

"AIDS is bad, sure. It's got nothing to do with me."

"Mr. Halsey. Philip. I hope you're not ignoring it. I hope you're being safe."

"Safe how?"

"A condom, Philip. Especially for anal sex."

I blinked a moment in confusion. Then I threw back my head and laughed. How thick am I? When her meaning hit me, it seemed obvious that Doris was leaving Stalls Associates, leaving *me*, because I was gay and therefore a noncandidate, after whatever interval she felt appropriate, to become her second husband. It explained her wariness with me after the familiarity she'd shown at Father's funeral. It was October, the metaphorical month of doom. But in my heart it was suddenly springtime, when animals mate and lovers marry and flowers bloom like madness. I assured her with aplomb that I wasn't homosexual.

"That's the officc rumor."

"I spread it! It frees me up for the real thing."

I knew from her frown that she doubted what I was telling her. I knew I'd have to prove it.

My work responsibilities had grown to include most of the duties of head trustee. I was setting day-to-day policy on equity sales and purchases; I signed the allowance checks to the office's many beneficiaries. But lately, with my head awash with Doris, I'd tried to simplify. I dumped all the proceeds of bonds that had come due into low-risk money funds. I sold every stock that was even mildly top-heavy rather than torment myself over quarter-points of added profit or loss.

On Doris's next to last day at the office, a Wednesday, my apathy turned outright destructive. I unloaded tens of millions of dollars' worth of utilities and blue chips, refusing to bear another minute their nonsensical ups and downs. By late Thursday, I'd drastically altered the portfolio profile of every trust Stalls Associates managed. I'd sold stocks held for decades into the roaring bull market. Our assets suddenly were seventy percent in cash, none of it sheltered, all of it languishing in low-interest accounts.

Alarms sounded family-wide. I'd exposed Stalls Associates to huge tax liabilites. An emergency trustee meeting was called for Friday evening. I was upbraided as a mental case, "a loose cannon on the foredeck of our ship of finance" (in the words of Evan Stalls, a yachtsman and toy soldier collector). Yet the trustees' fury was tempered by that day's steep

Dow-Jones decline. I was ordered to buy back, at the market opening Monday morning, every issue I'd sold; it appeared Stalls Associates would, by luck, end up making money on my irresponsible behavior. The date of that Monday was October 19, 1987. Some people remember it well.

The past is overrated. You can ignore it and thrive. To be happy one must live in the present like children and Californians. Seize the day. Take a chance. Tell your father's secretary that you love her. Which is what, during the drive to work on Monday morning, I impulsively resolved to do. In Newton I asked passersby where the AIDS hospice was and received responses of startling variety.

The hospice occupied a large Victorian residence on a pretty brick-paved side street. A dikey-looking woman welcomed me—Reeboks, crewcut, multiple earrings like industrial staples. She said Doris was upstairs. At my hesitance she offered to fetch her for me. "Not necessary," I said. "I embrace the danger."

I passed a common room where some young men were watching TV, some of them even laughing. A chairlift track ran along the stairs to hoist and lower invalids, the chair itself a heedful servant waiting at the top. The second floor had been remodeled into a series of cubicles opening onto a center hallway. I saw neatly-made narrow beds inside the cubicles, straightback chairs for visitors, and bureaus of a size bigger than you'd find in a motel room and smaller than you'd need at a place of permanent residence. "Doris?" The silence scared me. Then from a cubicle with a door half-closed came a hushed reply:

"In here."

I peered inside. I recoiled. "Jesus. Sorry."

"It's okay," Doris said. "He gets these bad headaches, and sometimes the medication just levels him." I made myself step forward, sweating in the high heat of the place. "I'm surprised to see you here," she said. "What's wrong? Philip?"

She was leaning over a bed, adjusting a damp cloth over

143

the forehead and eyes of a man naked from the waist up. Her hands were wet and red. Her hair was tied back with a rubber band. I fixed on her as an alternative to him—all knobby at the elbows and shrunken at the belly and ribcage as if fed on from the inside out. The man gave a sound. I couldn't help but stare. The cloth covered his face like those skewed black rectangles you used to see in seedy crime magazines, covering the victims' faces. He whispered, "Doe?"

She bent to his ear. "You feeling better, honey?"

"S'here?"

"A friend. He's helping today."

The man tried to cover himself. Doris draped his shirt over him. He quieted, presentable now. "I gotta go," I said.

He raised one hand—to wave goodbye, I thought, so I waved back. Doris smiled at my error. "Just shake."

His fingers were twigs in my grasp. "I'm Lyle." He pulled the cloth off his face with his free hand. His gaze took a moment to focus, aiming over my shoulder as if seeing someone I didn't.

"I'm Philip . . . Halsey."

"Philip," he repeated. "Halsey." Recognition lighted his face as no doubt it blackened mine. "Philip? *Philip!*"

"Lyle! Hey!" I shook his hand vigorously, my grin mirroring his, two skulls saying hello. It felt absurd to be looming over him flapping his hand like a lawyer with an accident victim. "How are you, man? Long time no see!"

Doris said, "You know him?"

"Platonically," I said quickly. Lyle, in the muddle of some medication, began to babble:

"Oh, your child, such a beautiful child! Gershom and Susie and everybody loved you after that. Sholem will love you someday, too." His voice went singsong. "*Philip Halsey had a son—*"

"The fuck!" I yanked my hand out of his grip and retreated into the hall. I covered my ears as "Philip! Philip!" resounded behind me like the reaper reading his list. Doris followed me:

"Get a grip! He's just confused."

"How long's he been your patient?"

"Lyle runs this place. Now he's sick, too. Maybe he'll die here, I don't know. Some want to be home for it, some want to be far from home. They should get their wish, at least."

"Know him well?"

"As well as I want to. It's hard when you get too close. Now go back in there and sit with him. It'll do you good."

"And what he said—"

"I don't listen when he's like this. I told you, he's in and out." She pushed me toward Lyle's door. I heard him murmuring my name, saw his head loll sideways on a jelly neck. The sight frightened me, for it seemed an apt summation of my past and future. To lie alone, trapped in my head, hollering "Philip, Philip"? I know destiny when I see it.

I panicked. I grabbed Doris and shoved her against the hallway wall. I kissed her, holding my mouth on hers as she fought in my arms like an animal. I pressed my pelvis hard against her so she wouldn't misunderstand me.

I let her go. I stepped back and watched her fury subside. Doris spoke in a choked whisper, "Get out of here."

"*You* will do me good. Only you. Not playing nurse to some goddamn freak." At which she struck my face with a punch that really hurt. And the blows kept coming, her fists streaking before my half-covered eyes like bees attacking me. After driving me to my knees, she stepped back to catch her breath.

"You frighten me, Philip."

"I would never hurt you."

"You just did."

I tasted blood on my lip. "I'm in love with you. Highly unsuitable, but there it is."

"You're just a boy to me, a boy that somehow got big. And trust me, you don't know me at all. I'm not what I seem."

"*I* am." I said this as a sort of symmetrical rejoinder, not intending much by it. Apparently it made sense to Doris:

"I'll consider myself forewarned."

"I just love you in the worst way, that's all I can say."

Her hair had pulled loose of the rubber band. Dark strands obscured her face like cracks in a photograph. When she flicked them away, my pulse skipped at the clear sight of her features and the deliberation that ruffled them. It is change in someone that I've come to believe is the sexiest thing there is. Whether the change is for better or worse makes little difference. Moral decline is as fetching as virtue if they exist in competition, an angel on one side and a devil on the other. Friction is the key. The friction makes a spark, the spark is alive, and vitality is what I crave since I rather lack it myself. Doris, disheveled and unnerved, but considering, yes, *considering* my insane proposal, was shooting out sparks like a turbine gone haywire. She'd either short circuit or generate powerful heat in response. I saw her soul expand with possibilities and their consequence. I couldn't have loved her more than then, no matter what her answer.

"You don't know me," she repeated. "There are things—"

"What? That you slept with my dad? To hell with him."

She half-smiled at my utter whiff. "How do you think I came to this hospice, Philip? I came when my husband was dying. He died here. Of AIDS."

"You mean he was—a swinger?"

"He contracted HIV through a blood transfusion—not that it makes a difference. And it's possible he passed it to me."

"No signs yet?"

"It may not show up for years." She backed away suddenly, appalled at herself. "How can I talk like this, to you?"

"And meanwhile, what? You wait it out alone?"

"I thought I ought to."

"I'll wait, too."

"That's stupid. Anyway, I'm too old for you."

"It's all the rage."

"I just buried my husband!"

This I had to respect. I stepped back with a courtly nod, prepared, out of customs of decency, to withdraw for the moment. "I am sorry. And I greatly admire the work you're doing here." I floated down the hospice hallway reveling in life's wonder. Doe (my pet name for her now) might be carrying the virus that causes AIDS: Loving her would be an everyday dance with mortality. I loved myself for wanting to risk it. The feeling was a first.

But when I turned at the top of the stairs for a last look at her, I was stunned to see that she'd slumped to the floor and was leaning wearily against the wall. Doe lifted her head, and in the brave flat tone of a man pleading guilty she offered a grim confession: "I work here because I *hate* it. I may spend my life at this, but I'll resent every second of it. Like I resented my husband. Philip, do you understand that?" She got to her feet and stood with her shoulders square and chin upraised, haughty in her disgust. "My husband fought so hard to live. He did it for me. He went without painkillers and medicine in order to be clear and active and loving for as long as he could. He suffered so much before he died, and all I felt was relief to be free of him." She gave a fierce shrug. "I work here, you see, for ridiculous reasons of guilt."

"Be guilty, fine. Your life doesn't have to end."

"You would say that. You have a cruel disposition, Philip. You're blessed, I suppose. Being invulnerable. Knowing you'll always prevail."

"That's rather severe."

Her laugh chilled me. "Not my description. It's how your dad always described you."

"As *cruel*?"

"It was affectionate, in its way. 'My dear little assassin,' is how he used to put it."

"That's just," I exhaled, "kind of astonishing."

"Doe!" sounded behind her. "Doe, come on, I need you!" She moved toward Lyle's room. "I gotta go," she said. "Gotta get busy saving my soul."

"Save mine."

"Goodbye, Philip."

"Tell Lyle I'll visit tomorrow. We have lots to catch up on, it's clear." Lyle had borne witness to major parts of my history; the least we could do was hold each other's hand and compare journeys past and future. "I'll be here bright and early," I called after her. "I want a mop and bucket ready and waiting. I want bedpans to empty and toilets to scrub. I want," as Lyle's door clicked shut behind her, "a fucking second chance!"

Shaken and distracted, I drove back to my parents' house, where, ever frugal, I'd been living since my return three years ago. Stalls Associates' trustees had ordered me to buy back today the securities I'd sold last week. Screw it.

Mother was reading in the library. I sat beside her on the sofa. The scene at the hospice had put me in mind of old times. I removed from my wallet the passport photograph of my grandfather, Philip Holscheimer. "Do you know the story behind this?"

"That's your father, of course. Around the time we met."

"Can't be. This man is middle-aged. This man is bald and jowly."

"David always looked distinguished. He was in his midthirties there, I'd say." She asked where I'd got it.

"From Father. He said it was of *his* father—somebody named Philip Holscheimer."

"If so, it's an extraordinary likeness. It quite resembles you."

"Don't tell me that! Is my face that fleshy?"

"It happens to men as they age."

I stood and began to pace. "If the guy in this picture is David Halsey, who the hell is Philip Holscheimer?"

"Excuse me?"

"Holscheimer! Holscheimer!"

"I worry about you sometimes, Philip."

I quizzed her, "Father was born a Jew, yes?"

"So he said."

"But he was a Halsey when you met him?"

"Yes."

"What about his parents? Ever hear about them?"

"His parents disowned him, you know that. It was one of those sad things that happen in families sometimes." Her eyes misted. "For as long as I knew your father, he carried a burden I couldn't relieve because he never shared it, until too late. It makes me cry to think about it."

"He shared it with me a long time ago. I never told you."

148

She nodded as if unsurprised. "That was cruel of you."

"Please don't call me cruel, Mother. I really don't want to be thought of that way."

Driftily, "I always felt so sorry for him." Here's one law of marriage: When there's nothing about your lover to love anymore, you must love him because he can't love himself. I pitied her for swallowing such bull, admired her for keeping it down.

Displaying the photo once more, I felt like a cop with a mug shot. "For the record: Who is this person?"

"He is my husband, David Halsey. The man I loved." She eyed me from under drooped lids, her expression proudly coquettish. "A girl never forgets."

I again studied Father's picture (it seemed now a perfect likeness) and recalled his long ago observation about it: "That man is dead to me. We killed each other." I felt reprieved, remembering this, for since Father's death I'd sometimes wondered if I hadn't murdered him, more or less, if I hadn't been self-servingly cruel at our reunion in 1984. It was a relief to think he'd killed himself many years before, when he'd buried his name and his past and his culture in order to be reborn in America.

I put the photo back in my wallet where I keep it to this day. I feel peace of mind whenever I look at it. Nothing matters eventually, is its reassuring message. Embracing this truth, I embraced another: I realized how bizarrely I'd behaved with Doris earlier. I stood no chance with her, lucky girl. Forget the past, despair of the future, was the lesson of the day—a prescription for mental health.

The phone rang in the foyer.

"Philip? Get me Philip Halsey!"

"It's me, Cousin Stalls."

"Who is this? I want Philip!"

"This *is* Philip." I knew what he wanted. Before he could fire me for not following orders about buying back the stocks

I'd sold, I preempted him: "I'm sorry, Cousin Stalls. The events of today have made me quit."

"I don't wonder," he said. "I shit, too. Five hundred points it fell! Five hundred points!"

"What are you talking about?"

"I'm talking about the stock market! I'm talking about a historic cataclysm. I'm talking five hundred bloody points!"

"I hadn't heard."

"Left early, did you? Too noble to gloat? Not me. I watched the bastard plummet, and laughed." Stalls laughed. "Oop. Spilled m'drink."

It began to sink in. "It fell five hundred points. Wow."

"Wow, he says. *Ho*! You're a cool one, Philip. You saved us millions, you know that. Your father would be proud."

I realized that my outlaw antics of last week, the massive sell-off I'd orchestrated out of despondence, had spared Stalls Associates from a stock market crash of epic proportion. Stalls Rayburn was still raving:

"You're a genius, son. Everyone says so. It's your show to run now. What's our next move?"

"Our next move?"

"The field is ours! Time to rape and pillage!"

"Hmm. I guess we let the dust settle. Our short positions probably went through the roof. Cashing those in should keep us amused a while."

"Short? You sold short?"

"As insurance, yeah." And out of pure apathy on my part— hedging our long positions had saved me a lot of worry. At the other end Stalls was giggling.

"It's too sweet. We made money on Black Monday."

"I suspect quite a lot."

"He suspects quite a lot. *Ho*! You're a hero, son. A god!"

There was a ruckus at his end. His voice sounded different. "I'm on my knees now, Philip. I'm kissing the phone. I've placed the phone on the floor and I'm kissing the phone . . ."

I looked forward to work the next day.

It passed in a blur. Secretaries, lawyers, and trustees applauded when I entered the office. Relatives sent flowers and witty telegrams. Stalls Rayburn took me to lunch at his club, introducing me around as "the man who saw it coming." A sober gathering, most of the club members had been financially creamed yesterday and were still in shock. I calmed them with my opinion that our nation, our system, our way of life, ultimately would prevail. Recession would come sooner or later, sure, but thanks to the shakeout of October 19th, it would be less than what we deserved. They raised their glasses to me. I've joined several of their companies' boards since then, and there's been a push to get me into politics.

I'm head trustee at Stalls Associates now. My annual salary is $200,000. Last year this was augmented with a $1 million bonus. The trustees know they must increase this in the future, if they want to keep me happy.

Our worth has exploded under my regime. We've made *Forbes* magazine's list of the wealthiest families in America two years running. Our investment strategies have become an art form for me, a means of self-expression. The vision I express is of precarious refuge. Money says it best.

When I got home from work that Tuesday evening, the day after the market crash, I noticed the cook's and housekeeper's cars were gone and an old MG was parked out front. I found Mother at the dining table tickling the skin of a clear soup with a silver spoon. I took my usual seat at the far end of the table, where a place setting had been laid as if for a banquet. Candelabras blazed between us. I heard sounds in the pantry. Mother wore a party dress. "Have some wine, dear."

I filled my glass.

"Forgive me for starting. We waited and waited."

"It was a busy day."

"Fulfilling, I hope."

"I made us all a lot of money. I won't complain."

"I hope you're tithing for church and charity. It benefits others, and ourselves as well."

"It's tough since tax reform."

Mother's white hair looked blond in the candlelight. For a scary instant I saw her as I'm sure Father had seen her when both were young: an elegant, uncomplicated girl who would be pleasant company. She said to me, "You'll do what's best, I know."

Such chat, on nights we dined together, was typical. Yet this evening's formality had a stagy air, fashioned toward some end. I resolved to let it happen; a sense of welcome anticipation was too rare in me to question. Candlelight glinted off my silverware like moonlight off moving water. In the curve of my teaspoon my reflected image was flipped upside down. The distortion told the truth.

There was a clatter in the pantry. Down with the spoon, up with the wineglass. When Doris Zuppa swept through the swinging door she seemed born of the red pool I drank from. She set a soup bowl before me. Her reflection on the surface of the broth was golden; on the silverware, pale peach. The reflections moved in unison as she touched my shoulder.

"Doris! Well!"

"Hello, Philip."

"Doris is here," Mother said.

Doris's hand rested at the base of my neck. Every nerve in my body aligned toward it like millions of Muslims toward Mecca.

"Your mother permitted me to make you both dinner. You're late."

"He had a busy day," Mother explained.

"I'm sure. Saving Stallses from themselves."

"And how was your day, Doris?" In her prime, Mother could subsist for days on cocktail chatter. The table, the candles, young people at hand—she'd found her bygone paradise.

"My day, Mrs. Halsey? A nice young man died in front of me. Then I had lunch." Stung, Mother returned to eating her soup. I'd turned at Doris's reference:

"Lyle?"

152

"No, just a drug addict from Roxbury." She looked across at my mother, exhaustion in her voice. "I'm sorry, Mrs. Halsey. It's just that so many die."

"I'm gonna go see Lyle tomorrow," I said.

"His condition is not dire, if that's your worry. He's much better now than when you saw him."

I was defensive. "I'll go. I want to go. I just couldn't make it over there today." I felt Doris's fingers clamp my neck imperceptibly, as if to let me know she could squeeze much harder if she chose.

"I know he'd like to see you. He was expecting you all day. You did promise you'd come. You should keep your promises."

"I plan to. From now on."

"All your promises . . ." I felt her breath in my ear. My spine actually tingled.

"Yes, ma'am."

Doris kissed my bald spot—a gesture so intimate, so brazen and yet demure, that I squirmed with instant arousal. I looked up at her. Her expression was both stony and creamy. It held challenge and sufferance and, I didn't imagine it, utterly inappropriate lust. I closed my eyes in grateful bliss, having found the perfect woman for me.

We're married now. The gossip it caused among my cousins was offset by relief that I wasn't completely alien to realms of human sentiment. As for Doe's family, the sour pill of her hasty remarriage doubtless was sweetened by the material fortunes of the match she'd made. Her former in-laws cursed us, however. I confess I'm bothered by this.

It's not superstition, exactly. But since getting married, I've experienced a sense of vulnerability quite new to me, a foreboding aroused even by the hurt feelings of people I don't know, as if their bitterness might bring down some cosmic retribution. Harmless occurrences, offhand words of criticism, resonate evilly in my mind. My fear comes in part from wondering if Doe carries the HIV virus. Years of relations with her late husband, before he was diagnosed, may have passed it to her. She's tested negative so far, but any minor ache or pain prompts our projections of the worst.

We practice safe sex most of the time. One of the times we didn't resulted in Doris's pregnancy. I worry about her health and much less so about my own. But it's the health of our coming child that stirs my deepest dread.

We know it will be a boy. I'd doubted the results of Doe's amniocentesis, but when I saw his dick on ultrasound, *hah!* I've already cleaned out a basement closet and begun stocking it with sports equipment. To further facilitate bonding, I've hired a Fenway bleacher bum to teach me the rules of baseball.

While cleaning out the closet I discovered all the weather notebooks I'd compiled as a boy—years' worth, stacked on a shelf, diagramming clouds, temperature swings, anniversaries of natural disasters, predictions for the future. It was poignant to see how much diligent effort I'd spent on something as fleeting as weather. The notebooks read like manifests of cargo ships sunk centuries ago. What treasure they once carried lay only in pointless nostalgia for those young days, like jewels, lost. Treasure like that is cursed. No good comes to men who pursue it.

One day late in Doe's pregnancy I was lying with her on our back lawn. She'd pulled up her maternity top to expose her naked belly to the sun. I imagined our baby warm in the sunlight and felt nicely warm myself. Doe had taken temporary leave from the hospice. I volunteer there two afternoons each month, doing laundry or mopping floors. Penance: Even I'm not immune to its call. Discussing events there isn't morbid for us, therefore. It allows us to ponder with detachment the potential sword over our heads and our child's.

Somehow Lyle's name came up. He'd rallied amazingly from the grim state in which I'd first found him, and had resumed his work as the hospice's reigning Florence Nightingale. This weekend he'd gone to visit his parents, to finally tell them about his illness and himself. "He's doing great," Doris said. "I really thought he was going to die that day you first visited. After you left, he got all talkative in that dreamy way some people do." She'd been with my father when he died, and indeed was unenviously expert in how people make their exits. "One of the things Lyle talked about was you."

"Strange to be the subject of someone's dying words."

"It was something to dwell on that wasn't the future. He told me about your life in those years you were away. He called you a terrified monster, but said you were worth saving. I think he had a thing for you—maybe he still does—and in a way he passed it to me." She laughed. "Don't ask me what I mean."

"I'm just glad it happened." I'd never asked her why she'd returned to me after I'd assaulted her at the hospice. It seemed impertinent to question a miracle.

"Most of the time it's nice when people get lucid at the end. They can make their peace or whatever." She paused. "Your dad was different."

"He just drifted, right?"

"No," she said carefully. "He sharpened some. Like, when the minister visited him—"

"The minister who baptized him? He came to the house?"

"Wasn't for long. Your dad threw him out, said he didn't want any lies. His words: '*No more lies.*' I felt awful, sitting there." Doe laughed without amusement. "The poor minister was mortified."

I sat up. "Are you gonna tell me Father called for a rabbi?"

"Nothing like that. He just looked over at me and asked, real clear, when would he get better. I told him he wouldn't get better. I had to be honest at that point. And he started crying. Very quiet and steady, tears running down like a runny nose. He did that for a long time, sitting erect, just staring and crying, like someone watching a sad movie. Till he died."

"Curious," I managed to say. "I wouldn't have pictured it that way." I fell back in the grass. I felt composed and anxious at once. With logic that fit but which I can't explain, Doe's story filled me with the absolute certainty that our child would be born afflicted, that he would die young, and that somehow it would be fair. The piece that makes the puzzle clear. The nail in the coffin. Mine.

Worse, way inside of me, I wanted the tragedy to happen;

wanted it to happen in order to set right my accounts. Crazy, I know. Not to mention monstrously selfish. In apology, I turned my eyes upward and spoke aloud to my son inside his mother, as if, though unborn, he could hear:

"The wind is southwest, David. I see cirrus clouds moving this way."

"Mare's-tails, tell him," Doe said.

"To the east, humidity over the ocean has created layers of altostratus, indicating precipitation somewhere."

"Tell him the forecast."

"The forecast?" I gazed westward beyond our back trees to the sky above streets and houses I couldn't see, the sky above, I imagined, young couples like Doe and me raising families in our American suburbs. I feared for us all, but a good weather-man never shows doubt. "Blue skies," I said after a moment. "I see blue skies today and tomorrow."